RIDE ME DIRTY

BRIDGEWATER COUNTY - BOOK 1

VANESSA VALE

ISBN: 978-1-7959-0029-4

This is a work of fiction. Names, characters, places and incidents are the products of the author's imagination and used fictitiously. Any resemblance to actual persons, living or dead, businesses, companies, events or locales is entirely coincidental.

Cover design: Bridger Media

Cover graphic: Period Images

GET A FREE BOOK!

PROLOGUE

ATHERINE

The hallway was dark, the pulsing beat of a new dance number thumped through the wall at my back as he held me there, trapped between the unforgiving plaster and his hot, lean frame. His lips were hard and dominant, demanding my surrender, even as I squirmed in his hold. He was the only man that I wanted to disembowel with my stiletto and fuck with equal need.

"Don't move." He pressed forward, his solid body pinning me to the wall, his rock hard cock a temptation I couldn't ignore as I ground my hips against him, trying to get closer. God, yes. More.

"Does this bossy shit work with all the girls?"

"Your pussy's all hot and wet, doll. Don't deny it."

His dark eyes met mine and the look I gave him should have withered his balls. Instead, it made him grin and I swear I felt his cock pulse. "Shut it down, doll. Every thought in your head. Work. Life. Everything but my dick pressed against you. Shut it the fuck down before I take you over my knee." I narrowed my eyes and was equally appalled and aroused. "You wouldn't."

The thin material of his suit pants was almost no barrier between us as I raised my legs and wrapped them around his hips like a woman in heat. I had no idea arguing would be so fucking hot. My skirt slid up and I rubbed my bare inner thighs against his hips, eager for more.

Lifting my arms over my head, he trapped my wrists in one hand, freeing the other to slide to my waist as he kissed my neck, licked it. Sucked on it. There was going to be a mark there come morning. I arched to give him better access as his fingers left a trail of heat on their way to cup my full breast beneath my blouse. He shoved the thin material up his calloused palms on my flesh. My hard nipple begged for his attention.

"Yeeees."

Holy shit. Was that me? I didn't recognize that voice. I'd never sounded that desperate to be touched, that needy. And work... what work? Nothing turned my mind off faster than a man gently biting my nipple. And not just any man. *Sam Kane.* God, he'd been a childhood crush, the star of my schoolgirl fantasies, but that had been fifteen years ago.

He'd been a boy then. Now, now he was *all* man and I was climbing him like a tree. We'd spent the past hour arguing and he instinctively knew how to push every one of my buttons. Instead of kneeing him in the balls, I was in the hallway of a public place letting him touch and taste and lick me.

"That's it. The only thing you should be thinking about is this." His lips claimed mine as his free hand slid lower, down my abdomen. His blunt fingertips slipped over my skirt to my thigh, then up, higher, and stroked along the lace of my panties.

His hand tightened around my wrists, his tongue plundered my mouth and two fingers nudged my panties to the side and slid into me. I was so damn hot for him I nearly came from that one rough thrust.

I couldn't stop the throaty moan that escaped me as he pulled his fingers free and fucked me with them again. He was opinionated, bossy and annoying as fuck. He even stole my cell to keep me from working. So why was I panting his name as he did what he wanted?

Grinding on his hand, I tried to get him to stroke my clit, to take me the rest of the way, but he broke off our kiss and bit my bottom lip lightly, just enough to let me know he was in charge. "Not yet, Katie. Not until I give you permission."

Permission? How dare he! I dripped all over his fingers.

My pussy clenched and he pulled back, thrusting twice more, ever so careful to keep his hand away from my clit. I moaned in frustration and he nibbled at my jaw. "That's the sound I want to hear from you." He fingered my clit once, with a swift, light touch that just drove me higher. I whimpered and he returned to take my lips, speaking against them as his fingers moved in and out of my wet pussy gently now, so damn slowly I wanted to cry.

He kissed me, hard, then unwrapped my legs from his waist, then moved lower. Letting go of my wrists he knelt in front of me and lifted my skirt to my waist. My lace panties he simply shoved to the side as he held me in place with one hand on my abdomen. The other he used to spread me open for his mouth.

"Oh shit," I murmured, staring at his dark head between my thighs, feeling his hot breath fan over my pussy.

I should tell him to stop. We were in the damn hallway of a bar. True, a back hallway, but anyone could walk in at any moment. I should behave like a proper professional and tell him no, tell him to wait until we were somewhere more private, more—

He sucked my clit into his mouth and flicked the nub with his tongue and I tangled my fingers in his hair. Head back, I didn't realize I'd closed my eyes until I heard a soft chuckle coming from my right.

Shocked, I turned to find the hot cowboy I'd met on the plane earlier watching us with an interested glow in his eyes. He leaned against the wall, arms crossed. How long had he been watching? Too shocked to move, instead I whimpered as my clit was released, then sucked back into Sam's mouth. Did he know we weren't alone? If he did, he was just too damn skilled to even think about being ashamed. Pushing at his head, I wanted him to move away, then with one little flick of his tongue, I tugged on his hair, holding him closer. I was on the brink, teetering on the edge of my orgasm.

The cowboy smiled and closed the distance. The hallway felt crowded. No, I felt crowded with two men paying *very* close attention to me. One guy had his head between my legs and making me come with just his tongue, the other blocking out the world with his broad shoulders. He lifted his hand to my cheek, then stroked his thumb over my bottom lip. "I see you've met my cousin."

Cousin? He grinned, then he kissed me, hot, wet and deep as Sam worked my wet pussy with his tongue, pushing me right over and into an earth-shattering orgasm.

As Sam got me off, his *cousin*, Jack, stifled my screams with a kiss. I was in deep, deep trouble here.

1

ATHERINE

Ten Hours Earlier...

"This is the captain speaking. We're in line for takeoff, but as you can see out the window, the weather isn't playing nice and the tower has put a ground stop on all flights. Not sure exactly how long this thunderstorm will hold us up. Looks like we'll be here for at least half an hour, folks. We'll keep you posted."

Great. Peeking out the airplane's small window, I could see the roiling charcoal gray clouds that prevented us from leaving Denver. I'd dashed from one gate to the far distant commuter area to reach my connecting flight in time, only to be waylaid like this on the tarmac. I glanced at my watch, then sighed. I didn't have time for this. Hell, I didn't have time to go to Montana, but I was going just the same.

Leaning back into the uncomfortable headrest, I shut my eyes and tried to breathe away my frustrations. I was up half the night finishing the depositions that had to be filed this morning, then spent another two hours closing out as many emails as possible. By the time I'd finished that, I still had to pack. I had nothing, *nothing,* that was appropriate for the Wild West besides a pair of jeans and running shoes, so after an hour of fretting, I just threw a little bit of everything into a bag.

I'd slept a measly two hours when the alarm went off at four-thirty, only to find the bridge from Manhattan to Queens was having overnight repairs and the traffic was backed up. Then airport security was long and I'd suffered the up close and personal pat down because of the titanium pins in my leg. When I had finally reached the gate, my boss had called to complain about my lack of face-time with my current client list. I wanted to make partner badly enough that I actually considered abandoning my suitcase and just heading into the office, but when my flight was called to board, I knew I had to get at least one mess in my life cleaned up. And now I was stuck in a thunderstorm.

As I tried to rub away the sandpaper feel behind my lids, I attempted the deep breathing techniques I'd learned in yoga class. The classes were supposed to be calming, but they never worked. I was never calm. And right now, the canned air inside this tiny airplane was getting hotter and hotter, sinking into my lungs, suffocating me. I was stuck and there was nothing I could do about it. Shit. I hated things that were beyond my control. I wasn't claustrophobic, but I felt trapped just the same. A huge clap of thunder shook the plane, just before rain pummeled the metal like a thousand tiny hammers. Was God trying to tell me something?

Breathe.

Breathe in slowly through the nose, hold it, hold it, let it out through the mouth. Breathe in...sandalwood and leather with just a hint of warmth I was sure had to be completely unique to *him.* I sat next to Mr. Cowboy Hottie and he smelled too good to focus on anything else—especially with my eyes closed. The scent wasn't cologne, soap maybe, and had me completely distracted. How could anyone concentrate on yoga breathing when Tall, Dark and Handsome and I were bumping shoulders?

I'd almost swallowed my tongue when he'd walked down the narrow aisle, put his cowboy hat in the overhead and took the seat beside me, all but folding his large size into the small space. He'd offered a quick smile and a polite hello and opened his book. I'd been texting on my phone at the time, but my thumbs had frozen in place as I ogled him. Blatantly. I figured I owed it to all womankind to look my fill as my heart started once again.

He had fair hair that was a little long and curled at the ends. Combed, but untamed. His eyes were equally dark and piercing, but the way his full lips quirked up at the corners indicated he wasn't as intense as he seemed. Tanned skin proved to me he didn't work in an office. As did his big hands with short, well kept nails and a fascinating play of muscle that shifted just beneath the surface. Strong hands that made a woman beg to be touched. Most importantly, no wedding ring either.

I was a total perv thinking about my seat mate like this, but holy shit. He was pumping out the pheromones or something because suddenly all I could think about was climbing on his lap and taking him for a ride. My brain had stalled and my ovaries had taken over.

There weren't any cowboys in New York. And I had to admit, there was nothing like a man whose size and corded muscles were brought about by hard work, fresh air and sunshine instead of daily trips to the gym. No man could wear a snap button shirt, a pair of jeans and worn boots like a cowboy. And this man? He was *all* cowboy. Holy hell, I'd always thought the urban businessman was hot, but they were pale weaklings in comparison. They might be able to make a billion-dollar deal over lunch, but I'd turn a blind eye if they tried to get me in bed. But Mr. Hottie? He could ride and wrangle me into submission any day.

Since I wasn't going to tell him that, I glanced at my watch again. Three minutes had passed since the captain's announcement. I should use this dead time to my advantage. Bending forward, I tried to reach my bag, but the seats were too close together. I had to lean sideways to do so only to find the side of my head bumped into Mr. Hottie's rock-hard thigh. Rock hard and *warm* thigh.

Abruptly, I sat up and flicked a gaze his way. "Sorry!" I blushed furiously and bit my lip.

Oh shit, he had a dimple. He smiled, showing off that perfect indentation in his right cheek and I just stared at it, my mouth open. He had a five o'clock shadow, and I wondered if his dark whiskers would be soft or scratchy. Would he run them across his lover's skin? Use that slight abrasion to tease the inside of my thighs before tasting me with his—

"No problem. Anytime," he murmured, his voice deep.

Was he insinuating I could put my head in his lap *anytime*? Did that mean he wanted me to...

My eyes dropped to his lap and I quickly observed those well-worn jeans molded him in *all* the right places.

Mortified I was ogling his very large package, I looked away, not before he winked and grinned.

Trying to keep on my side of the arm rest, I used my foot to hook my bag and pull it forward—bending in ways that I *was* thankful for hours of yoga to achieve—to finally get my hand on my laptop and cell phone and setting them on the tray table. Taking my phone off airplane mode, it rang right away.

Wanting to silence the ring, I answered it.

"Don't think you can sneak off and sell your uncle's property without me knowing."

Just hearing Chad's voice grated on my already frazzled nerves.

Since I'd blocked his cell number, he was probably calling from his office. Why couldn't he leave me alone?

"I don't need to sneak. I'm selling my uncle's house. Now you know." I kept my voice low so I didn't bother anyone else.

"And keeping the profits for yourself? Not going to happen, sweetheart."

"I'm not your sweetheart, Chad. I doubt I ever was," I grumbled. When I'd discovered him in bed with his paralegal, I had to assume she was his sweetheart instead.

"You are my wife and that entitles me to half of that inheritance."

I glanced out at the rain dripping down the window. My emotions were the same as the sky, dark and threatening to unleash. "You've been in bankruptcy law too long. We're not married anymore. Which means you're not entitled to anything."

"Says the woman who, four years in, still hasn't made partner."

Wow, that was a low blow. Chad had been made a junior partner in his firm after eighteen months, and never let me forget it. I glanced at Mr. Hottie and discovered he was looking at me, watching me with an intensity that made me squirm in my seat. Was that concern on his face? God, I didn't need him to hear me fighting with my asshole ex-husband.

"Chad, I'm sitting on a plane and can't talk. We have nothing else to say to each other. Stop calling me."

I hung up and just stared at my cell. We'd been divorced for almost two years and he was still trying to fuck with me. It had been a stupid marriage and the fallout from that hasty mistake still lingered.

Yoga breathing wasn't going to calm me down from this one so I had to shift my thoughts. Work. Work would make me focus on something besides my lying, cheating, backstabbing asshole of an ex.

I pulled up the brief I was writing and got to work while Mr.

Hottie read his book. After a few minutes, an instant messaging box appeared in the lower corner of the screen.

Elaine: Saw your name pop up. You're there already?

Me: Stuck on grounded connecting flight in Denver. Thunderstorm.

Elaine: That sucks.

There was a minute delay, then she wrote again.

Elaine: Remember your primary mission! Find a hot cowboy and engage in monkey sex!

My eyes widened at the message in the corner of my laptop's screen.

Flicking my gaze toward Mr. Hottie, it didn't appear that he had noticed my friend's racy note. The type was small and while the seats were close together, I had to hope he was extremely nearsighted. And focused on his book.

Me: Waste of time. I have too much work to do.

Elaine: Famous last words of a woman who desperately needs an orgasm. Chad was an asshole with a pencil dick. You need to find a man to rock your world.

Elaine had no filter and that's what I loved about her. She didn't mince words. What she said about my ex's dick was probably true. Sadly, I'd only been with him so I didn't have tons of dicks for comparison but he certainly didn't know how to use it. As for having my world rocked, well, I doubted that was going to happen anytime soon. I was too busy. Work, work out, more work. Occasionally, I slept. As Chad so kindly pointed out, I hadn't made partner. Yet. If I wanted to be one, I had to clock the hours.

Me: Sex won't get me that partnership.

Elaine: You've got warped priorities, woman, if you think you can't have both. You think Mr. Farber doesn't get laid?

I wasn't sure if I should laugh or throw up in my mouth. My boss was in his sixties and far from attractive. And a misogynistic hard ass.

Me: Funny.

Elaine: A one-night stand. I'm not saying marry the man, just fuck him. Then find another and fuck him, too.

I sighed, trying to figure out how I was going to find a guy to fuck. I wasn't exactly a model with my short stature and curvy body. And one-night stands weren't exactly my style. How did one go about doing that? Was I supposed to just walk up to a guy at a bar and tell him I wanted to have sex? Drink and act silly until the man made a move, go home with him and sneak out as soon as we were finished? The whole thing made me uncomfortable. The thought of turning from an uptight, workaholic divorcee who'd only ever slept with one man into a sultry seductress in the wilds of Montana just didn't seem feasible.

Me: Fine. The first man I see when I get off this plane, I'll just ask to fuck me. That should work, right?

I could have sworn I heard Mr. Hottie grumble, but when I glanced at him, he was still reading.

Elaine: It's worked for me. Seriously though, find a hot Montana cowboy and go for it.

Mr. Hottie still hadn't moved and I inwardly sighed. This conversation was not something he needed to see.

My phone chimed.

Me: Gotta go. Mr. Farber is texting.

Elaine: He can text? LOL.

I rolled my eyes and shut down the messaging window. Grabbing my phone, I read my boss's text.

Farber: Hearing date for the Marsden case changed to Tuesday. In your absence, Roberts will take over.

"Fuck," I whispered, my hand tightened around the phone case until my knuckles were white.

I stared at the words and wanted to throw the phone across the plane. Eric Roberts was vying for the same partner spot I was and he was a total asshole. Besides having a law degree, he had a Masters in brown-nosing and a PhD in poaching cases. I'd been gone half a day and he was already taking my biggest case. I could only imagine what he'd accomplish in the week I'd be gone.

Normally, I would have smiled politely and bitten my tongue. But not today. I muttered to myself as I answered Farber's text with a polite recommendation that he send Martinez instead. Martinez, at the very least, thought with something other than his penis. Roberts had fucked his way through the entire paralegal department and had now moved on to the receptionist in the orthopedic office on the fourth floor. "Roberts. You asshole. Think you're going to ruin me."

"Do you always talk to yourself?"

I turned my head and looked up at Mr. Hottie.

"I'm sorry?" I asked, confused. My brain was still processing how my career was going into the toilet at an alarming pace.

"I just wondered if you always talk to yourself this much."

Reality crashing back in on me, I blushed hotly, then looked away, seeing the flight attendant work his way down the aisle.

"Oh, um. Only when stressed." I laughed drily. "That means yes. I talk to myself all the time."

A little V formed in his brow, then glanced at my computer. "Stressful job?"

The flight attendant came to our aisle. "Since we're stuck here, drinks are on us, folks. Beer, wine, liquor?"

"Liquor," Mr. Hottie and I said it at the same time. We looked at each other and smiled.

"Name your poison then," the flight attendant replied, pencil and paper ready, looking to me.

"Vodka tonic," I said. "Make it a double."

"Same," Mr. Hottie replied.

When the flight attendant moved down the line, Mr. Hottie turned back to me. "You seem to need that drink."

"Or ten," I muttered.

"That bad?" he asked.

"Drowning my problems in alcohol is the only thing I can do at this point. Since I've been on this plane I've had a phone call from my ex, an IM from a coworker and a text from my boss. On top of that, I won't make my appointment in Montana on time." I waved my hand toward the plane's window and the water streaking down it. "I can't go back to New York and, after months of hard work, they're giving my case to an ass—" I bit my lip. "An associate because I'm stuck here."

Mr. Hottie's dark gaze was focused on me. Like a laser. It was as if he couldn't hear the storm brewing outside or the screaming baby two rows back or the conversation of the couple in front of us. He was listening solely to me, and the attention made me hot all over. I had to fist my hand at my side to keep myself from finding out just how soft his hair would feel sliding through my fingers.

"Being stuck isn't so bad," he told me.

I arched a brow, my gaze flying to his lips as he spoke. Lingering because I couldn't seem to remember that it was impolite to stare. "Oh?"

"Mmm," he murmured. "Being stuck with a beautiful woman? Every man's dream. Aren't I lucky?"

2

I licked my lips and forced myself to face forward, like a reasonable, logical woman. How many times was this man going to make me blush?

"I'm Jack, by the way."

I licked my lips again, the slight dampness left by my tongue teasing me with possibilities as I answered. Maybe this was how it worked, picking up a man. Maybe Elaine was right. Maybe I could do this. "Catherine."

Jack shifted his legs so they stretched out into the aisle a bit. "What is it you do that has you so stressed?"

I considered lying for a split second, but my instincts rebelled at the thought. If he couldn't handle a woman with a brain, I wasn't interested anyway. "I'm an attorney."

"My cousin's a lawyer, too. I usually crack jokes about lawyers, but I don't think they pertain to you."

I laughed and nodded my head. "Yeah, I've pretty much heard

them all." I tugged at one of my wayward curls. "And I'm blond, too, so I'm pretty much doomed in the bad joke department."

"So what's the big issue that has you so wound up?"

He placed his hands on top of the book in his lap, interlaced his fingers, clearly settling in to the wait. I just looked at him for a minute, trying to figure out why he cared.

Perhaps he sensed my thoughts, because he said, "Look, talking to you is much more enjoyable than my book. Besides, we've got nothing else to do. You might as well tell me." When I still paused, he said, "What happens on the plane, stays on the plane."

"I thought that was only for Vegas," I countered, then grinned. "Fine." I turned so my back was against the bulkhead of the plane and I faced him.

"My biggest issue is that I'm up for partner and an ambitious co-worker took over my biggest case. I've been gone—" I glanced at my watch and did the math on the time change. "—six hours and he's poaching my clients."

"Partner. That's impressive, especially for someone so young."

I frowned and looked at him carefully. "Thanks. I'm not that young and I don't think you're old enough to claim old age just yet."

"I don't dare guess a woman's age. My mother taught me better manners than that, but I'm thirty-two."

"Then I'll just say you've got a few years on me." Five to be exact, but he didn't need to know that.

"Like I said, impressive."

I looked down at my short nails. "Making partner has been a goal for ten years. I've worked my tail off and the thought of the jerk in my office stealing the partnership out from under my nose makes me want to strangle things."

"You always wanted to be a lawyer?"

"Yes."

"Why's that? Someone in your family put away for a crime they didn't commit?" The corner of his mouth tipped up and his dimple appeared. I stared. I couldn't help it. I wanted to kiss him there, find out what his skin tasted like.

Holy shit. Elaine was right. I needed to have sex. The long dry spell since my divorce was making me lose my mind. "Um... no. My father's a lawyer. My mother's a lawyer."

"Following in their footsteps then."

I thought of my parents. Not warm and fuzzy, not loving in general. But, they'd put me through college and law school so I shouldn't complain. "I guess. I never really thought about it. It was always just what I was going to do." I'd said enough about me. Time to turn the tables. "What about you? What do you do?"

"I'm a rancher."

"What does that mean exactly?"

"Ever been to Montana before?"

"When I was young. My uncle lived there."

He gave a slight nod. "I run a horse ranch."

"I pegged you for a cowboy."

"I pegged you for a city girl."

I glanced at my laptop and my phone. Saw my crisp white blouse and slim jeans. "Yeah, you can take the girl out of the office, but you can't take the office out of the girl. Right?"

He looked at me for a minute. "I don't know about that. Maybe you just need to try."

I bristled at his words, then sighed. "Believe me, it's not that easy. I've been trying my whole life." I'd done everything the books said to do to relax. Beach vacations. Yoga. White noise machines and a monthly massage appointment. All they got me was stacks of unanswered emails, a sore shoulder from too much *downward dog*, nightmares about buzzing insect attacks and complete mortification as a stranger rubbed lotion into my less than perfect body while pretending not to notice how utterly far from perfect it truly was.

The flight attendant brought our drinks on a tray, handed me mine, then Jack his.

I took a swig of the frosty drink and felt the alcohol sit on my tongue, then slide coolly down my throat.

"Headed to Montana to visit your uncle?" he asked, adept enough to know he needed to change topics.

"My uncle died a few months ago."

"I'm sorry to hear that," he murmured.

I offered a small shrug. "I was twelve the last time I saw him. My parents had some kind of falling out and we never went back."

"Falling out?"

I took another sip of my drink. "They never told me. I asked, believe me, but they wouldn't say. Surprisingly, he left his house to me and I'm going up there to clean it out and sell."

"It's in Bozeman then?" If this plane ever took off, we'd land there.

"No, Bridgewater. A small town about two hours away." Was it my imagination, or did his eyes narrow at the mention of the town? I was about to ask, but the buzzing of the airplane's intercom system drew my attention.

"Okay, folks." The captain's voice boomed through the overhead speaker, preventing Jack from saying more. "While you can see it's still raining, the storm's headed east and the runway's open. We're fifth in line for takeoff."

The flight attendant came around then to collect the cups. Not wanting to waste the drink, I downed the rest in two gulps before handing it over. I had no choice but to put my laptop away since the tray table had to go up. We started to move then, slowly up the line as one plane took off after another. Quicker than I expected, we were in the air and the effects of the alcohol were kicking in.

Now I was buzzing on both his scent and the vodka, and all I could think about was finding out more about this sexy cowboy.

"I never thought to ask, but are you heading home to your ranch in Montana or is it in Colorado?"

"Montana," Jack replied. "Born and raised. I was in Denver for business. My turn."

When I frowned in confusion, he said, "My turn to ask a question."

"Okay. Shoot." The alcohol was filling me with a warm fuzzy feeling and I knew I wouldn't normally open up like this. But what the hell? I'd never see him again anyway.

"I don't see a ring. You mentioned an ex?"

"Divorced. You?"

"Never married."

"Girlfriend?" I was dying to know and the liquor was loosening my tongue.

"No. Boyfriend?"

I shook my head. "Not enough time. My friend says—" I cut off my sentence, realizing I was sharing too much. It didn't matter that I would never see this man again once the plane landed in Bozeman. It didn't matter how easy he was to talk to. There were some things a girl just didn't share. Like the fact that I needed wild and crazy monkey sex up against a wall and at least five orgasms.

"Your friend says...?"

I looked at his gorgeous face, his very broad shoulders, the entire package. I could just tell him what Elaine said. I could proposition him, tell him I wanted to have monkey sex with him. He was single, had said I was beautiful. While I doubted we could be in the Mile High Club—the bathroom on this plane was barely big enough for one, let alone two people—we could easily find a hotel near the airport when we landed. I bet he was good, too. Really good. Those hands, the cock that was clearly outlined in his jeans. He could easily rock my world. The words were right there on the tip of my tongue. *Are you interested in a one-night stand?*

Elaine *so* would have done it. But I chickened out. Hell, I didn't want to be rejected. Chad had found me lacking. If Jack did, it would be crushing.

"Nothing." How could I get out of this conversation? Bathroom. Every woman needed to *powder her nose,* even at 35,000 feet. "Um, if you don't mind, could you let me out?" I pointed toward the back of the plane.

Jack unbuckled his seat belt and stood, moving out of the way in the narrow aisle so I could walk to the back of the plane. When I shut the lavatory door behind me, I laughed out loud. How anyone had sex in a space this small was beyond me. It was so tiny and definitely unsanitary. I took a second to look at myself in the mirror, to see what Jack saw. My blond hair was wavy and hit my shoulders, my bangs long and combed off to the side. It was somewhat untamable in the east coast humidity, which wasn't all that great for the corporate look. I'd resigned myself to that a while ago, but I was pleased that the color didn't come from a bottle. I tucked it behind my ears and wiped my fingers beneath my eyes, ensuring my mascara hadn't moved downward.

"You're talking to a hot guy. He's interested in you, regardless of your quirks and insanity. He's not going anywhere so get out there and talk to the man." I stared at myself, then frowned. "Yeah, right. As if he'd be interested in me."

Working my way back down the aisle, I discovered Jack asleep. He had his head tilted back, mouth open slightly. God, what would those full lips feel like on mine? I couldn't keep standing in the aisle and stare, but I didn't want to wake him because he looked completely out. The only way to get to my seat was over him. Putting one hand on the seat back in front of me, I lifted my leg and winced as I stepped over his. God, he was big. I put my foot down on the floor, leaning my weight on it to bring the other one over, but my legs were too short. I'd totally miscalculated and I was stuck straddling his thighs. Oh shit.

Jack startled and shifted his legs, which lifted my toes off the floor. I lost my balance and fell forward, my knee landing on the empty seat next to him, and my bottom landing firmly on his lap. This, along with my little squeak, had his eyes popping open. Instinctively, his hands went to my waist. Being as small as I was, his thumbs brushed the bottom curve of my breasts which were pressed to his chest.

My eyes widened in alarm as I felt the hard length of him at the juncture of my thighs. If the thin barrier of our clothes weren't in the way, that hard length would be sliding through my folds right about now. Naked, I could ride him like this, right here on his lap, my breasts pressed to his chest, his mouth just out of reach. If I just lifted my chin—

Our eyes met, held. I was frozen in his lap, like a frightened rabbit. My brain completely shut down and I couldn't move, couldn't talk. I had no witty comment to smooth over the situation. No. Not me. First in my class on the trial advocacy team, and I couldn't think of a single thing to say. Nope. All I could think about was getting a complete stranger naked. Monkey sex.

His gaze narrowed and was filled with heat and intensity. His pale eyes were a stormy gray. Like the clouds beneath us. I shuddered.

I finally got my voice back. "Oh um, shit." I leaned toward my seat and tried to lift my other leg over, but his hands held me in place. "Sorry, I... um... didn't want to wake you." I knew my face was fifteen shades of red, but there was nothing I could do about it.

He grinned then, easily lifting me so that I could swing my leg over and turn to sit back in my seat.

"Anytime, Catherine, anytime."

I could still feel the squeeze of his hands on my sides, the hot

—and very hard—press of him on the backs of my thighs. Mortified, I felt my cheeks burning and I looked everywhere but at him. With fumbling fingers, I put my seat belt on. God, how does someone survive such embarrassment? I had to do something, anything, so I didn't have to talk with him anymore. Elaine had wanted me to throw myself at a man. Well, I'd done it. God, not that I wanted the plane to crash or anything, but I could die of embarrassment right now. Nothing had changed. I sucked at flirting. Always had. Give me a rule book or a procedure manual and I was a genius. But this? Flirting and sex? Yeah. Not so much.

"I... um... I better get back to work." While the words were for Jack, I spoke to the seat back in front of me.

In my periphery, I could see he lifted his chin once in acknowledgement, pressed the button on his chair to go back the measly two inches and closed his eyes once again. I could look at him unaware. He wasn't flustered like I was. He wasn't embarrassed or mortified. It had been nothing to him. *I* was nothing but an amusement on a delayed flight.

To me, that was the closest I'd probably get to riding a cowboy in this lifetime.

When he shifted in his seat, I turned away, afraid he would open those intense blue eyes and see me staring. After the falling in his lap incident, I couldn't be caught ogling.

Hooking my foot to pull my bag out once again, I spent thirty minutes typing up the remainder of the brief. With Jack sleeping, I was able to forget my blunder and focus, glad that I couldn't get any internet or cell service on the plane. My work insanity was at a minimum, but my to-do list simmered in the back of my mind. I might be in radio silence, but that didn't mean my world wasn't falling down around me. I could only imagine what I'd be in for when I got to Bridgewater.

3

ACK

"How was your trip?" Sam asked, tossing his pen onto his desk.

I never could understand how a man could work at a desk all day. But that was my cousin, and it made him happy. I thought of Catherine from the plane and realized she and Sam probably had a lot in common.

"Uneventful." I hung my hat on the coat rack by the door, then settled into one of the chairs in front of his desk. I'd gone to Denver to sell one of the quarter horses. While it hadn't been necessary to meet the buyer in person, sometimes it took a face-to-face to close the deal. The arrangements for transfer from my ranch to the one in Colorado could be handled by phone. "The return flight, though, was anything but."

Sam leaned back in his chair and put his boots up on the antique desk. *You can take the boy off the ranch, but can't take the ranch out of the boy.* "Did the plane hit another bird?"

"What?" I realized he was referring to a flight a few years ago when, on takeoff, a bird had hit the windshield of the plane and the pilots had aborted the flight. Not fun. I could laugh about it now, but I'd been stuck at a hotel by the Denver airport overnight because of a damn bird. "Shit, no. Thunderstorm this time, long delay, but that's not it. I met someone."

Sam's fair brows drew together and I could practically feel the judgment oozing from his skin. "Oh, yeah? Who's going to be in your bed this time?"

"Don't give me your bullshit, Sam, about having no-strings sex. She's just in town for a few days and looking for a good time. She's from New York. I sat beside her on the plane. Talked with her for awhile. Practically the whole time we were delayed a friend of hers was messaging her, telling her to find a hot cowboy and have some fun."

Was that a grin teasing at the edges of Sam's mouth? "I don't know how you find them, Jack."

"She needs me. Her pussy needs me. I can't just walk away." I sat down in the chair opposite my cousin in his big, fancy lawyer's office and couldn't keep the happy grin off my face. "One, she's sexy as hell. Curvy, blond, and strung up so tight she'll probably pass out the first time I make her come."

"I don't need to know." Sam was shaking his head now, but there was laughter in his eyes. Which was good to see. He hadn't quite forgiven me for costing us the woman he wanted us to marry all those years ago, before he left town. Sweet Samantha Connor. She'd been eighteen at the time and everything Sam wanted. What he wanted, I hated: innocent, sweet, dependent. Needy. I'd felt myself suffocating the closer Sam got to proposing. Hell, I'd only been fucking eighteen myself. I'd refused to marry her, she'd cried a river and married the MacPhersons six months later. Sam left town two weeks after the wedding and stayed gone for more than a decade.

"Hell, cousin. If anyone needs to get laid, it's her."

I grinned, thinking of her computer and cell and instant messaging and her full inbox and... hell, the seventeen other things she probably had going through that pretty head of hers. It was amusing to see her so intense and serious. On the plane, I'd had a semi since I first sat down and had to pull out my book to try and cover it. When she'd gotten up to use the lavatory, I'd enjoyed the view of her curvy ass as she walked down the aisle, which had only made me hard as a rock. I'd had to sit there, eyes closed and think about mucking out stalls and root canals to will it away. But when she'd surprised the shit out of me and tried to climb over my lap, I instantly imagined her riding my cock up and down, shifting her hips to get herself off as she fucked me. There was no question she'd felt how hard I was for her as I savored her warm curves beneath my hands, the soft feel of the underside of her breasts, her thighs pressing into mine the instant before she leapt off.

My cock stirred at the memory alone. Her body... lush and round. Perfect.

Now Sam's brows winged up. "Haven't seen that look on your face in awhile. That good, huh?"

I nodded and grinned, envisioning Catherine's blouse as it strained from her full breasts, her blond curls, the soft weight of her thighs on mine, her surprise at being caught straddling me. "Hell, yeah. That good."

Sam leaned forward and picked up a softball he had on his desk and started tossing it up in the air. We were on a summer league through the recreation center, and Sam liked to keep his hands busy. "If she's that good, then she's better than a quick fuck."

I shook my head. "I'd be game for more, but she just wants sex. Lots of sex. Needs it, in fact."

Sam caught the ball and looked at me, wide eyed. "How the

hell did you learn that from the plane? And don't tell me she actually said that to you."

She'd been about to, that's for damn sure, but she'd changed her mind. I'd watched the battle rage behind her expressive blue eyes, and nearly groaned with disappointment when I saw the cool, logical mask she wore drop down to hide her desire. "I peeked at her instant messaging conversation with a girlfriend. She was practically ordered to have a fling. She's divorced and looking for a good time."

Sam narrowed his eyes. "Why would she need a fling? What's wrong with her? If she's as hot as you claim, she should have men lined up wherever she's from."

"New York. And nothing's wrong with her." She was one perfect little package with curves I itched to hold again. "She's just got a type-A personality focused solely on the corner office. Uptight. Conservative. A lawyer, just like you."

"Ah, one of those." Sam had walked away from a big-time partnership in San Francisco, very similar to the one Catherine so desperately wanted, for the slower paced life in Montana. No more eighty-hour work weeks for him with his private practice.

"She's wound up tight. Real tight." I steepled my fingers. "From the IM conversation, I'd say she hasn't gotten any in awhile. If we got our hands on her, she'd probably go off like a rocket."

"We?"

"Yes, *we*," I countered. "She's not Samantha and I'm not eighteen anymore. I know what I want now."

Sam stiffened. We didn't talk about what happened all those years ago. It was a sore subject. Fuck, it was a huge fucking elephant in the room and it never went away.

"She wasn't the one for us," I added, referring to Samantha. "We weren't the men for her. She's married to the MacPhersons. Happy."

The town of Bridgewater, Montana was founded on the

principals of plural marriage. Two or more men for one woman. Back in the 1880's, when our great-great-great grandfather came to the United States from England, he—along with a few fellow soldiers—established Bridgewater as a safe refuge. They believed in the custom that two men should protect and love a wife. Together.

I didn't know the full story, but they'd served in the small, now extinct country of Mohamir that followed this custom; men who believed in sharing a woman. Protecting her, cherishing her and loving her in a way that kept her from ever being alone was their sole purpose. If one husband died, she had another to take care of her and any children. While it seemed to many outsiders to be chauvinistic, the lifestyle was designed with the woman in mind, with the woman the center of every family. Those original tenets set by our ancestors still held today. While not everyone in Bridgewater married this way, it was commonplace and understood. Sam and I, we'd grown up with it—we each had one mother and two dads—and wanted that kind of marriage for ourselves.

Sam dropped his feet to the floor with a thud and leaned on his desk. "Jack—"

"We're grown men. Let's stop acting like pussies about this. It's not about Samantha Connor any more. We were too young. Hell, I was eighteen and shaved once a week."

I ran my hand over my jaw, which was covered in a heavy five o'clock shadow. "What did I know about having a wife?"

"You're ready for one now?" he eyed me closely.

"I know you left because of the fallout with Samantha and I know why you finally came back—to find The One. It's time we found our bride."

He could have found a woman in San Francisco and settled down, married her. But he hadn't. He wanted a Bridgewater marriage. He just hadn't been ready before. Now, he was ready. We just hadn't found the right woman.

"And you think this woman on the plane is her?"

"Fuck, yeah. As soon as she straddled my lap on the plane, I knew then she was going to be in my bed. More."

His eyes widened. "Do I want to know why she was straddling your lap on a fucking commuter plane?"

I couldn't help but grin, reliving the sight of Catherine's stunned—yet heated—look. I'd had my hands on her, saw the flare of attraction and desire in her eyes. I wanted her again, on my lap was just fine, but without any clothes between us. I wanted to be able to see what color her nipples were, feel the weight of her breasts in my palms, watch them bounce as she took me for a ride, my cock buried deep in her sweet pussy. *Shit.*

I would have her. I knew it the moment I sat down beside her and picked up her clean citrus scent. When her pale eyes met mine, I saw the desire there. I'd felt sucker punched. Lightning strike. Name the cliché. I hadn't wanted a girl this badly since I was a scrawny twelve-year-old. And that hadn't worked out so well. But Catherine was a full-grown woman with perfect breasts and rounded hips. She was a little thing, but she was all woman. Soft. Curved. Aroused. Oh, hell yeah. I'd seen that look in a woman's eyes before. She'd been just as hot for me as I'd been for her. But she'd panicked and shut me down.

I didn't know her last name. Hell, I didn't know much. But Bridgewater County was a tight community and she was coming here. I was sure I could find her.

I adjusted my cock. Again. Having a semi for the past four hours made it uncomfortable to sit, but thinking about how she could've gotten herself off just riding my thighs on the plane wasn't helping.

"That makes it even worse. We fuck her, she gets the one night stand that she wants, then goes back to New York," Sam countered.

"The conversation with her friend only proves that she's not going to stay."

"Shit, man. You need to chill," I told him, shaking my head. I told him a thousand times to loosen up and the women would flock to him. Seemed he was even more uptight than the woman on the plane. I kept hoping one would come along and inspire him to unleash the fighter I knew lurked within. No such luck yet.

He gave me the finger. "You want me to fuck a woman I barely know and walk away? That's not how the Bridgewater way works, jackass. I want a woman between us that we're going to keep. Not fuck and wave farewell."

"Start by helping me find her. Talk to her. I'll bet you fifty bucks you'll take one look and be hard as a fucking rock."

He waved his hand toward the door. "I'll think about it. Now, get the fuck out of my office."

"There's only one problem." I didn't get up as he wanted.

Sam gave me an impatient look, waiting.

"Based on that IM alone, she's on the prowl. That means she might choose to fuck some random asshole just to get her jollies. If she wants hot monkey sex—" I held up my hand at Sam's raised brow. "—Her friend's words, not mine, we just need to ensure we're the men—the only men—to give it to her."

Sam sighed, ran a hand over the back of his neck. He wasn't just two years older, he was bigger than me. Taller and broader, he'd played football in high school and college. He'd wanted off the ranch all his life and I was just thankful he'd returned to Bridgewater to settle. Besides the whole Samantha fiasco, we'd been burned by women who either wanted us for our money—the ranch wasn't small and Sam did extremely well as a lawyer—or, for one night, interested in being in the center of a Kane cousin sandwich.

But I had a feeling about Catherine, a feeling she would love being taken by two men, love being touched and fucked and kissed by both of us. But convincing the uptight, New York attorney of that? Shit. That was probably going to be more difficult than I wanted to believe, and I would absolutely need Sam's help. He was the dark, brooding, intense one. I had a feeling Catherine would go for the quiet reserve my cousin offered before she would take a chance on a player like me.

Sam set the softball back on his desk and frowned. "Fine. I'll help you find Airplane Girl. But right now, I have work to do. Are we finished?"

I knew when to stop pushing. Until he met Catherine, I wouldn't be able to convince him. She'd be the one to do that.

I stood to leave and gave him a wave as I walked toward the door. "I know, I know, get the hell out."

Now I just had to find Catherine and figure out a way to introduce her to Sam. One look, and I was confident he wouldn't be able to walk away from her. No fucking way. Getting Catherine into bed with both of us was going to be a bit harder, but neither of us ever backed down from a challenge. And what a hot, enticing challenge she was.

4

CATHERINE

"How long will you be in town?" Cara Smythe asked. I'd found a note with her phone number and the house key tucked beneath the knocker on Uncle Charlie's front door when I arrived.

She grew up on the property next to his and we'd played together as kids when I would visit. I remembered her with red hair, freckles and a blue bike with streamers on the handlebars. God, I had wanted a bike just like that, but living in New York— and with my parents—didn't allow for one, or a puppy, or running through the sprinklers on a hot July afternoon. I remembered Cara as always smiling and happy, whether we were jumping rope or sneaking around after her older brother and his friends. Her parents were equally likable and I always envied their loving relationship. *My* parents were the complete opposite —spending Christmas on European cruises instead of in front of the tree—and I remember wishing I could stay in Montana forever. Instead, after the summer when I was twelve, I never went back. Life moved on and Cara was married now and lived in town.

"I have a ticket for next Wednesday, but if I get things wrapped up sooner, I'll change it."

I had stopped in town and picked up a few groceries and coffee so I could survive. Charlie's house was on five acres two miles out of town and I'd figured the cupboards would be bare. I'd figured right.

It made no sense to stay in a hotel when the house was now mine, at least it was officially once I signed the papers. I wasn't picky about where I slept—I could sleep standing up—and staying here was one less thing I'd had to plan while trying to get out of the city. I stood in the kitchen and it was just as I remembered it. Yellow walls, orange laminate counters and dark wood cabinets. Faux brick linoleum covered the floor. It was like stepping back in time, especially holding the phone that was attached to the wall, cord and all. My cell was charging by the coffee maker, but completely useless without any reception. I had no idea there were places in the US that had no cell service. Sure, the top of a mountain or in the middle of a desert maybe, but I was in Bridgewater County, Montana. It might not be heavily populated, but it *was* populated. Didn't people want to use cell phones around here?

"Why would you want to leave early?" she asked.

I sighed and glanced at the rooster clock over the stove hood. I'd been up thirteen hours and I was feeling it.

"I've got to get back to work." Just checking my email while waiting in line at the rental car counter had my blood pressure soaring. Mr. Farber hadn't taken Roberts off my case. That meant the longer I was gone, the less chance of getting it back.

"No, you don't. I know you lawyer types, working sixty hour weeks."

Sixty? Try seventy-five.

"It's Montana in July," she continued. "Let's have some fun, like when we were kids."

I pulled a loaf of bread and some peanut butter out of the grocery bag.

"God, Cara, we are *so* not kids anymore and a bike ride or climbing a tree doesn't do it for me now."

"When *was* the last time you rode a bike?" she countered.

I thought back. It had probably been her bike with streamers.

"You're married and I'm... well, I'm a workaholic."

Cara laughed through the phone. "The first step is admitting it. That's why I left the note, so you wouldn't stay holed up in that house working. And, being married does not mean the end of fun." She giggled. "The opposite, in fact."

I had an idea where her mind was going and it only made me a little envious. She had a man who made her laugh at just the thought of being with him. As for Chad, the rat bastard, he was a waste of time and brain power.

"How did you even know I'd be here?" I asked, changing the topic.

I walked to the fridge, put the milk inside, the phone cord stretching as far as it would go. There wasn't any food in the fridge besides an opened box of baking soda, a bottle of ketchup and five cans of Charlie's favorite generic cola. I wasn't sure if it was because someone cleaned out the perishables or not. I remember Charlie was a horrible cook, so it was possible he didn't keep much.

"Are you kidding? Everyone knows everything that goes on around here. I'm sorry to hear about Charlie. I liked him a lot. But I'm glad you're back."

Yeah, Bridgewater hadn't changed much since I was a kid. The main street was quaint with local shops. I drove past the lawyer's office so I knew where it was, but it was hard to get lost in such a small town. The mountains were to the west so there wasn't even a chance of getting turned around. As I was driving, those going the other way raised one finger on the steering wheel in greeting, stranger or not. It was a Montana thing I'd forgotten, but I liked it. I liked how people were nice, even to those they didn't know. That didn't happen in New York. It was cutthroat and fast paced, no one slowing down enough to wave to anyone else. No one ever looked up from their phone. But in Bridgewater, things were different. Cara, who hadn't seen me in... fifteen years, knew I was back and wanted to connect right away. It was startling for me. Unusual.

"I'd love to see you. Come out with me tonight."

I thought of my meeting for the following morning with Charlie's attorney, plus all the work I had to do for the office. My laptop sat as dead as my phone on the kitchen table. No internet at all. I'd searched for a cable or something, anything to indicate modern technology, but the house phone attached to the wall— with a dang cord—was all I had to connect me to the outside world.

I might be able to get the details of the sale wrapped up quickly, but not in one meeting. Plus, I had to empty the house, of Charlie's personal effects to be ready for sale. The man had lived in the house for forty years and it showed. I had my work cut out for me. I mentally groaned at adding another to-do to my already overloaded list.

Besides tackling the house, nothing else would get done here. I had to find a coffee shop or something where I could go online to work. I took vacation days for this week, but that meant nothing. *Vacation* didn't exist for those wanting to be partner. I still had work to do or Roberts would have *all* my cases by the time I returned. I could only imagine how my emails were piling up. I went to my cell, checked it for service. None.

"Okay, sure."

Placing the bag of coffee grounds by the coffee maker, I folded the brown grocery bag and wedged it between the fridge and the counter with about twenty others.

"Great. Then let's meet at the Barking Dog at eight."

"The Barking Dog?"

"It's a bar on the east end of Main. No excuses."

I looked around the kitchen and realized it was going to be awfully quiet by myself. There were no honking horns, no police sirens. There weren't even any street lights. A night out couldn't hurt, especially if I made good progress with the attorney in the morning. "All right."

"Great!" I could hear her pleasure in her voice.

"Hey Cara?"

"Yeah?"

I glanced at the rooster clock once again. "Do any of the coffee shops have wifi?"

If I could whittle down my emails, then I'd feel better spending a few hours with Cara.

"There are two in town and I'm sure they have it. But I think they're both closed by now."

"It's four in the afternoon!" Shit. Shutting the fridge door with more force than necessary, I wondered how a coffee shop stayed in business with those hours.

"They open at five a.m. though."

Five. I could do five. I was on east coast time anyway and could get that brief emailed to my boss before he even arrived at the office. After that, I could get in a few hours of work before my meeting at ten.

"I'm hanging up now so you don't change your mind. The Barking Dog. Eight o'clock."

After putting the phone back on the base on the wall, I went over to the coffee maker and grabbed the pot to fill at the sink. Some people might survive on junk food. I survived on coffee.

 ATHERINE

"Since you own the house, you should stay, or at least keep it and use it for vacations," Cara said as she stirred her straw around in her drink.

The Barking Dog was more brewpub than dive, with a wall of booths, high top tables and the original bar that had a mirror behind it and a brass rail. The owners had done a fantastic job of making it look like a Wild West saloon, but without the spittoons and poker tables.

I'd joined Cara and her husband, Mike, at one of the booths.

When I'd received the first email from Charlie's executor, I'd recognized the name immediately. Sam Kane.

God. *Sam* fucking *Kane*.

I'd been surprised, for he was only a few years older than me, but if he were one of the few attorneys in town, it was logical for Charlie to use him. But *Sam Kane*. It had been a simple school girl crush I'd had on him, furtively glancing at him whenever he'd hang out with Cara's brother, Declan. They'd been in high school together and I remembered, when I was at Cara's house, them making tons of food and eating it all while watching movies.

I'd been the outsider, just visiting from New York, but I'd been —gah!—all knobby knees and braces. I hadn't even discovered hair product to tame my wavy hair back then. I hadn't even had boobs. As the friend of a kid sister, I knew they didn't even take notice of me. Why would they have? The last summer I'd come to visit I'd been only twelve. Twelve! What high schooler even glanced at a twelve-year-old? When I never went back to Bridgewater for the summers anymore, Sam Kane slipped from my mind.

But now...now he filled my every thought. Was he as cute as I remembered?

"Earth to Katie," Cara sing songed.

I blinked, refocusing on my friend and her husband. It was weird to hear that nickname again. I was *never* Katie to my parents. I'd only been Katie when in Bridgewater.

While Cara was a petite redhead with peaches and cream complexion, Mike was built like a football linebacker and was quite tan. If it weren't for his quick smile and the tender looks he sent his wife's way, I'd be a little intimidated.

I spun my vodka tonic around on the cocktail napkin. "It's not mine yet. I have to sign for the deed tomorrow."

"Whatever," Cara replied, waving her hand. "You lawyers and your official signatures. It *will* be yours."

"It does feel weird *almost* owning property so far from home," I replied.

"You could make this your home. With that property free and clear, it would be cheaper than living in New York."

I almost snorted out my drink. "*Anything* is cheaper than New York," I countered.

Mike grinned.

"I live in a shoe box apartment, but I'm never there except to sleep."

Cara looked up at her husband. "See?"

I glanced between the two of them. "What?" I asked, a little worried.

"You work too hard," Cara offered. "You need to live a little."

"Got a boyfriend?" Mike asked.

I felt myself blush, but hoped the soft lighting hid it. I thought of Chad, the asshole. "I have an ex-husband and that's enough."

"You can't let one guy ruin it for you." Mike pointed at me. "You're young, smart, beautiful. Maybe it's the guys in New York. What are they called, metrosexual?" He took a swig of his beer. "What does that mean anyway?"

Cara and I laughed.

"I'd think Sam Kane is looking for a partner," Mike commented.

I stared at him, wide eyed. "A partner?"

"You're both attorneys. I'm sure you could easily find clients here instead of a big firm that only allows you to sleep."

Mike was a rancher and while his hours catered to livestock and chores, his pace of life was vastly different than mine. There was no commute to work. No rush hour. No overtime or deadlines. No IM's, no texts from upset bosses, no overloaded inbox. Just big skies and cows.

"Katie thought you meant a different kind of *partner*," Cara clarified, her mouth turning up into a grin.

Mike looked at his wife confused for a moment, then understanding dawned. "I vouch for Sam, Katie."

"Good to know," I mumbled, taking a sip of my drink. Elaine wanted me to have wild monkey sex. Cara was clearly matchmaking, and Mike was a job recruiter. I hadn't even seen Sam since I was twelve and it was like my friends were a committee that gave me a rubber stamp approval to work with, and more importantly, fuck Sam Kane.

"Sorry, I'm late." An attractive guy with blond hair came over to the table, leaned in and kissed Cara. On the mouth. Was that a hint of tongue? And she let him. No, and *Mike* let him.

What. The. Hell?

My drink was halfway to my mouth and I froze, my eyes going from New Guy to Cara to Mike and back.

New Guy whispered something in Cara's ear and she looked up at him adoringly, as if he were... Mike.

Mike nudged Cara with his elbow and all three of them turned to stare at me.

"I told you she didn't remember," Mike said.

Cara laughed. "Katie, you should see your face!"

I flushed and felt like I was left out of some kind of joke.

"Um... yeah, well—"

New Guy shook his head. "I'm Tyler, Cara's other husband."

Mike and Cara slid over to make room for Tyler in the booth. He moved in beside them, Cara wedged happily in the middle. One dark, one fair, one red head.

"Holy shit," I muttered, and took a big swig of my drink. I waved down the waitress and gave her the signal for another round.

Cara laughed and cocked her head to the side. "You really don't remember, do you?"

"What? That you have two husbands?" I leaned in and whispered the last, afraid someone around us would hear. "I would have remembered if you told me, I promise."

Mike shook his head. "You don't remember that Cara has two husbands or that most women around here do?"

"Most women don't—" I opened my mouth to disagree, but closed it. Frowning, I looked around the bar, then past it to the families seated farther away in the restaurant. There were a lot of tables with a woman, kids, and—two men. Not every table, but enough to make me swallow. Hard. Holy shit. I glanced at Cara and her men again. "But Cara, your parents—"

"You remember my mom, obviously, and my dad, Paul."

I nodded, for I'd played at their house often, had lunch. Cara's dad even fixed my bike chain once. Charlie had bought a red cruiser bike for me that last summer.

"You've met Frank before?"

"Yes."

"He's my other dad."

"You're other... He ran your ranch. I... I thought he was the foreman." I remembered Cara's parents and the foreman, vaguely, and from the perspective of a twelve-year-old. I never saw Cara's three parents together, that I could think of, but that didn't mean anything. My parents were only together for work functions and charity dinners, at least until recently. They'd begun to travel together when I was in high school. Cruising the Mediterranean, wine tours in Burgundy, African safaris. Without me. I'd always felt like the afterthought, hell, the mistake. They'd ignored my existence as much as possible, making time in their busy schedules to sit in the crowd during my prep school, and then college graduations. When I'd graduated from law school, they'd been on a cruise in the Bahamas, but sent an email congratulating me. I'd never seen them touch, or cuddle, or, frankly, act like they liked each other at all. Cara and her husbands were making me extremely uncomfortable, and, if I were completely honest, a bit envious.

Cara nodded. "Frank does run the ranch. But it's *their* ranch."

"But you—" I pointed between the three of them who seemed very comfortable with this topic. They weren't joking, they weren't anything but blatantly in love.

"If you look around, you'll see it. Not just the bar. The town, too."

I glanced at the other tables again, looking at the women, half expecting to see each of them with a flashing neon sign over their heads that said *I have two husbands!*

"It's illegal," I added, then felt bad. Shook my head. "Sorry, but this is all so crazy."

The waitress brought the drinks then and I was glad for the refill. I could feel the effects of the first drink, and welcomed the heat that spread through my stomach.

After taking Tyler's order, the waitress left and all three of them watched me expectantly. And they weren't wrong. I had questions.

"Does every woman in Bridgewater marry two men?"

All three of them shook their heads. Mike lifted his arm and placed it along the back of the booth behind Cara. He was at ease, comfortable. "Not everyone. Some women only marry one man, some marry three. It's not that it's unusual, it's just... *normal* for us."

I wasn't sure how polyamory was *normal*, but the way Mike and Tyler looked at Cara, I could see they were happy.

"Yeah, but..." I fiddled with my fingers, thinking about sex and how that worked.

"The sex?" Cara asked, as if reading my mind. She grinned, then glanced at one man, then the other.

"Watch it, babe," Tyler said, putting his hand on top of hers.

"I was going to say—" She glanced slyly up at him. "—that it's awesome. What woman wouldn't want two men to take care of her? You should try it!"

Cara wiggled in her seat, her cheeks pink with a blush of excitement.

"It's not for everyone," Tyler murmured.

I laughed. "I think I need to work on one man first. Two? That's a bit of a stretch for me."

"There's a guy at the bar eyeing you," Cara said, tilting her chin in that direction.

Without any subtlety, we all turned to look.

I recognized him immediately, then sighed. "That's not a man, that's your brother," I grumbled.

Cara laughed. "Still, he's waving to you and wants to say hi."

I sighed, slid across the seat. "Wait, do he and another man share a wife?"

"Single," Cara replied.

"I'll go and talk with him and get the next round."

Mike held up his glass, almost full. "Take your time. If Declan's not the guy for you, just wait. You're going to be like a flower to the bees, sweetheart."

I gave Mike a doubtful look.

"Don't do anything I wouldn't do," Cara giggled.

Wedged between two men, both of whom were her husbands, I could only imagine what she *did* do.

6

 ATHERINE

As I walked over to Declan MacDonald, I thought about what I'd just learned. Two men! Cara was married to both Mike and Tyler. God, how did that work out? Obviously, I'd heard of threesomes, but that was like... a one-time thing, right? Get it on with two hot guys, check off that fantasy from the bucket list, then get back to reality. Follow the rules. Find a good man, settle down, get married. But Cara was *married* to two men. Married. As in forever. Did they all sleep in the same bed? Or...

"Hey, Squirt." Declan pulled me in for a big hug. He was as tall as I remembered, but he'd filled out. With similar coloring to Cara, no one would doubt they were siblings.

"God, Declan, it's been a long time." Even though he'd been older, in high school and had me and Cara tagging along on occasion, he'd always been nice to me. Kept an eye on me when I knew my parents didn't. I didn't have a big brother and as a kid, that's what I always thought of him to be.

He pushed me back, put his hands on my shoulders and looked me over, then frowned. "No ring on your finger? What's wrong with the men in New York?"

What was it with everyone these days? Why was everyone so damn worried about my status as a single woman? I was divorced, not dying of some incurable disease. Did I look that lonely and desperate?

Tilting my head to the side, I looked at his hand. "No ring for you either. Haven't found a wife... and another guy to share her with?"

His smile slipped a little and his eyes turned serious. "You didn't know?"

I shook my head and bit my lip. "Didn't remember. Or, when I used to come, too young to understand. I just found out, really." Glancing at Cara, she was smiling at something her men said, their heads angled close to hers. It was obvious they were together. "You don't mind? Cara, I mean?"

Declan let me go, then directed me to sit at one of the bar stools. "I'd rather *not* think of Cara with any man, but Mike and Tyler are good to her."

"Two?"

"That's the way it is in Bridgewater. It's the way it's been for over a hundred years. Hell, the area was founded on the principle. It's accepted, embraced even. No one divorces."

"But two!" I repeated, waving my hand in the air. "Seriously? It's not even legal."

"I heard you were a lawyer." As if that explained my answer. "Only one of them actually marries the woman. The rest is just a mutual understanding."

"Some understanding. I couldn't stand my ex-husband. Why would I want two of them?"

Declan grinned. "You might be surprised, Squirt. We're raised to put women first, in all things. We protect them, cherish them,

43

love them. Take chivalry and amp it up about ten times. When a man finds the right woman, there's no going back. Can you say that about your ex?"

I laughed then, thinking of Chad. Chivalry? Protection? "God, no."

"You've just found the wrong guy. *Guys.*" When I looked skeptical, he went on. "You like sci-fi movies?"

I shrugged, confused by the change of topic. "Sure." I couldn't remember the last time I was at the theater, but I could envision Star Trek and little green men.

"It's like a tractor beam. When a guy gets his sights on his woman, she's pulled right in. He doesn't waver, doesn't doubt. Never cheats, never sways. It's... powerful." He glanced up and his smile widened. "Kind of like that."

I turned to look and found a man I didn't recognize approaching us. A hot, gorgeous, virile, stunning stranger. Damn, he was hot. He nodded at Declan as he took the barstool next to me, but his attention didn't waver for long. With a short, "Dec," his intense gaze returned to me.

"Hello. I'm Sam Kane." He held out his right hand like a perfectly reasonable human being.

Me? I froze as the name registered—slowly. *Sam Kane.*

Sam was big and broad like a football player with the good looks of a cover model. His nose had a slight crook to it, giving him an air of danger, or at least a bar brawl or two. He screamed cowboy, and yet his dress was more corporate than Carhartts.

His greeting moved through my mind about as fast as chilled molasses through a straw. I knew I was supposed to say something, but damn, I couldn't seem to remember how to talk. This was even worse than my FUBAR on the airplane with hottie cowboy Jack. Yeah, that was fucked up beyond all recognition. Now, I was two-for-two in embarrassing myself with sexy men. Go me.

Sam Kane had been cute when I was twelve. Now, holy fuck. Beam me up, Scotty.

With a chuckle, and a protective hand on my shoulder, Declan made the introductions. "Sam, you remember Katie Andrews from... God, when we were in high school. Katie, this is Sam."

I placed my much smaller hand in his large palm and finally remembered to breathe as he gently squeezed. Tingles crept up my arm and I hoped he'd never let go. This was the teenager I'd mooned over? Shit, he was *not* a teenager any more. He was like sex on a stick with a fucking cherry on top.

"Hi. I...I think...you're the attorney handling my uncle's estate? Charlie Willis." That was good. I didn't fumble that too much.

His gaze narrowed and I watched the lightning quick analysis going on behind his dark eyes with helpless fascination. "Yes, and you're my ten o'clock meeting tomorrow."

Nodding, I stared at the way his dark hair curved to cover half of his forehead, inspected the sharp lines of his face and hard jaw until my attention rested on his full lips. They looked hard, but firm, as I imagined his kisses would be, aggressive, urgent, dominating to the senses.

Wow. My mind went right to the gutter, but what woman could blame me? He'd filled out, matured. Turned out to be... gorgeous. I pulled my hand free and cleared my throat. What was it about hot men in Montana? Was it the water? All the fresh air and sunshine? Hormone-free milk? Turning to face the bar, I took a sip of my drink and tried to recover. "Ten o'clock. Yes. Nice to see you again."

Nice? Seeing him again was like a cattle prod to my libido.

Turning to Declan, I gasped to discover the stool empty. Looking around quickly, I found he'd taken my place at Cara's table, where he, along with Cara and her husbands raised their glasses in salute, as if giving me permission to flirt with Sam. Alone.

Apparently, Sam saw them, too. The soft sound of his chuckle of amusement made my heart race. "Looks like I have been given permission to buy you a drink, Katie. What do you say?"

"My glass is full." Oh, yeah. Great answer. Idiot. I felt my cheeks heat, but couldn't think past the facts of the moment. Airplane Jack, with his blatant masculinity, playboy smile and rock-hard body had pushed me so far off kilter that I had no chance of resisting Sam.

I took a deep breath, let it out. I could do this. I can talk to a hot guy without being a complete idiot. I had a law degree. If I could defend a case before the most ruthless of judges, I could talk to a hot guy in a bar. And it wasn't just any guy, but Sam Kane.

Maybe it was because of Airplane Jack that I decided to let go with Sam. I'd blown it with him—epically—and God would not put this hottie in my path to fuck up twice. In the same dang day.

God, he was dressed in a navy suit and tie. His cream-colored dress shirt and crisply ironed dress pants said this man was like me, a tough professional, a driven individual who paid attention to the details. Add his movie star good looks and the fact that he was acting interested, and it was safe to say he was scrambling my brain. I'd never been any good at off-the-cuff flirting even when my brain was actually working.

"A suit and tie. I thought I was the only one overdressed," I commented. I wore a skirt with four inch heels to a bar. In Montana.

He grinned then. With those straight white teeth and the little turn up at the corner of his mouth, yeah, my panties just got soaked.

My cell phone chose that moment to buzz in my purse. Resigned to the inevitable, I reached in my bag, pulled it out. I slid my thumbs over the screen, once, twice. I read the email. The effects of the liquor were gone and my brain turned back on, set to hyper mode.

"Excuse me," I said to Sam, but had my eyes on the cell and the two paragraphs about work that couldn't be ignored. I shouldn't have come to the bar, taken time off. God, why wasn't there internet at Charlie's house? I wouldn't have missed this. Shit, if I could just get this one thing resolved...

Sam's large hand wrapped around my wrist.

"Let it go," he murmured in my ear.

I shook my head, focused on the status of my case, the brief that needed to be filed, the injunction. "I can't. It's an important email and I just need to—"

"Work. Yeah, I know. I'm a lawyer, too. Remember? Trust me, it can wait."

My back stiffened as I looked up at him. His dark gaze was focused squarely on me. No phone in his hand, no eyes on a damn palm-sized screen. He wasn't focused on work. He was focused on me.

"It *can't* wait. Do you have any idea what's going on in my little world while I sit here with you?" I lifted the phone and shook my head.

"Yeah, I have an idea. Your work is always at DEFCON 2, which means you're mobilizing the troops in your mind for some all out war with the other party. I can practically see the smoke coming out of your ears you're thinking so hard."

Yeah, that about summed it up.

"How many drinks have you had?"

I frowned. "Two."

He looked me over. "And you're still wound up tight. You need to chill the fuck out."

Now I was pissed and I stood. Just because I lived with a metric shit ton of stress didn't mean my work wasn't important to me. Cara and those men might vouch for Sam, but he was a jerk. "And if I were a man, I'd be considered career driven, not wound up. Look, Sam, I don't need you to tell me about my job. About what to do."

He grinned again. Cocky bastard.

"Yeah, I think you do. And I wasn't being sexist with my comment. Women have more balls than most men, and you do the same job in hot-as-fuck heels." He glanced down my legs to the ruthless heels I usually wore. "I was the big city lawyer once, too and I'd been wound up so tight I was going to have a heart attack before I turned thirty." He studied me with that intense dark gaze again. "I think you need someone to help you shut it all down."

"But—"

Sam grabbed my cell from my hand, held it up in the air so the only way I could reach it was to climb up on the stool. I wanted the phone back bad enough, but I refused to be baited.

"We can debate all night. Hell, it would be fun and a serious turn-on, trust me. But it's nine at night. Even later in New York. Work can wait."

Reaching behind him, he slipped my cell in his back pocket. I eyed his ass.

"Try for it. Trust me, I'll like it."

Another fucking grin. Cocky bastard.

I narrowed my eyes.

He circled his finger at me. "This prickly lawyer routine probably scares people away. I find it fucking hot. That outfit is your armor, right? Let's dance."

He didn't give me a chance to argue further, only tugged me onto the small dance floor and put his hands at the small of my back. We were close. Real close. I could smell him, not clingy cologne, but soap that smelled like the outdoors and pure unadulterated male.

A swat to my ass had me startling.

"Chill. The. Fuck. Out."

I narrowed my eyes, ready to strike him dead with a zinging one liner.

"That look is only going to get you kissed. *Dance.*"

I took a deep breath, let it out. I had Sam Kane's hands on me, his thumbs stroking over the top swell of my butt. Speaking of my butt, it was warm where he'd spanked me.

"I've killed people with my stiletto before," I warned him, beginning to move.

"No doubt you have a whole string of dead bodies in your wake." He shifted his hips, slid his leg between mine, making my trim skirt ride up my thighs. I was practically riding his thigh, which was not bad at all.

"The thing is, doll, that's another turn on."

I laughed then, trying to cover up my growing desire. Who knew arguing was hot as hell? And that swat, it made my ass tingle and my pussy wet. My libido was singing, no, screaming at me to press my body chest to chest and thigh to thigh. I wanted his hands to move a little lower, to settle on my ass. I wanted to bury my nose in his neck and breathe his subtle scent into my lungs. If I were being totally honest, I wanted his cock pounding me into oblivion so I didn't have to think about all the bullshit I was dealing with in New York. I wanted to forget about work, and life, and the asshole back at the office who was, most likely, stealing clients from me at this very moment.

"Stop thinking, doll, or I'm going to have to spank you again."

———

SAM

"You are a misogynistic asshole," she muttered.

My hands pressed her into me more firmly. She couldn't miss the feel of my cock, rock hard, against her belly. Even with her killer heels, she was tiny. Well, she wasn't tiny, she had lush curves that felt incredible against my palms. Her breasts were mashed into my chest and I swear I could feel her nipples harden.

I didn't know why her attitude got me hard, but it did. She wasn't mild. She sure as hell wasn't meek. From the emails we'd shared about her uncle's will, her work schedule was insane. It had taken her a month just to rearrange her appointments and get work on board for this trip. Her throttle was wide open and she refused to slam on the brakes. That made me want to be the one to slow her down.

"Let's go, doll."

I tugged her off the dance floor, pulling her with me across the bar and down the hallway by the restrooms, then around a corner to a small area by the emergency exit. The lights here were dim, the music quieter. While someone might come upon us, no one would think to go past the bathrooms unless there was a fire.

I pressed her up against the wall, my hands at her hips holding her in place. Even with the dim green glow of the exit sign, I could see her eyes widen.

"Asshole, definitely. Misogynistic?" I shook my head, looked at her parted lips. "I love women. Even ones who are pricklier than a cactus. But like I said, you need to chill the fuck out and I'm the one who's going to make you do it."

"Oh really? And how is that? Gift certificate for a massage? Free yoga class? Yeah, I've tried it all."

I slowly shook my head. "Yoga? Hell, no. Although I bet you look damn hot in those tight little pants. You need to come a few times. That should loosen you up."

"And you're the man to do it?"

"Absolutely. Right here in this hallway."

She thought I was all talk. Hell, no. She needed to come on my face. That would take the edge off. She looked around, but we were definitely alone. "Here? No way. I don't do stuff like that."

"That is fucking obvious."

"You might know what you're doing in a courtroom, but this?" She waved her hand between the two of us, although I didn't give her much room to do so. "You might need to pull out a text book or something. It isn't working."

Not working? I bet her panties were soaked. I was going to find out, because while she might like to be in charge, it wasn't going to happen.

"I warned you, doll. Don't push my buttons because I'm going to push yours." I slipped one hand down between her legs and I could feel the heat of her through her skirt and panties. Yeah, her panties were soaked. "I'm going to push this button... right here."

I tapped at her hard, little clit and she gasped.

"I hate you," she said, her voice breathy.

"Is that so? Your pussy seems to like me just fine."

She rocked her hips into my palm and begged. "Please."

"That's my girl," I murmured, leaning into the task before me.

7

Now
CATHERINE

"Oh my God." As the orgasm wore off and reality returned, I hastily pushed down at my skirt as Sam rose to his feet. Using the back of his hand, he wiped his mouth, which was, oh, wet from my arousal. He'd made me come with just his tongue, well, and his cousin's attentive kisses, the rough brush of Jack's whiskers, his dirty, filthy words he whispered in my ear. My pussy still quivered with little aftershocks of pleasure.

Standing—no, looming—before me were two gorgeous men who, together, gave me the best orgasm of my life. *Oh. My. God.*

They were both grinning, of course. Assholes.

It was completely unlike me to allow a guy to drag me to a back corner of a bar and then go down on me. Yeah, that had never happened before. I'd never even *fantasized* about it before. I would now, for the rest of my life. I didn't even *like* Sam, but he was so fucking hot and he somehow made me crazy. Crazy in lust.

"I liked swallowing the sounds of your pleasure, sweetheart," Jack said, voice cocky.

I felt my cheeks heat and it wasn't from coming all over Sam's face. I couldn't meet his gaze. I knew he was staring at me. I *felt* it.

When he'd come upon us, he hadn't been upset catching me in such a compromising situation. No, he hadn't even been upset with his cousin. He'd been eager to join in. Join in! With his relaxed stance, one shoulder against the wall, I had no idea how long he'd been watching Sam lick me, how long he'd seen me tugging and pulling on Sam's hair to get him to move right where I wanted him. I'd been too far gone to care that he'd come over and joined in. And when he'd kissed me, oh shit. I'd never come like that before.

Sam elbowed him as he ran his tongue over his lower lip. "I did all the work."

"Yeah, and you got to taste her pussy," Jack grumbled.

Sam grinned. "Damn straight."

"You're cousins?" They looked nothing alike. Sure, they were both big, but that was where the comparison ended. Jack was fair while Sam was dark. Jack seemed lighthearted and Sam was the serious one. The rancher and the lawyer.

"You got it. Our fathers are brothers," Sam said. He lifted his chin toward me. "And you're Airplane Girl. Jack told me all about you. Except that Airplane Girl is really Katie Andrews."

"Katie Andrews who used to come from New York to visit... ah, it all makes sense now," Jack replied, running his fingers over his jaw. I could hear the rasp of his whiskers even over the muted bar music. "I wanted to find you and introduce you to Sam, Catherine, but we're all *well* acquainted now."

My hands came up and covered my eyes. "I... I can't believe I just did that."

Sam took a step closer, dropped his voice to a dark whisper. "What? Come all over my face?"

That broke me out of my embarrassment. I pulled my hands away and narrowed my gaze. "God, you are so crude. I need to get back to Cara," I whispered.

"Cara Smythe?" Jack asked. "Yeah, she and her men left."

"What?" My eyes widened. "They...they left?"

Jack brushed my hair back from my face. "They must have thought you were in good hands."

"Yeah, mine," Sam said, stroking the backs of his fingers down my arm. I swatted it away.

"You just started a little early," Jack added. Why did they have to stand so close? "See, sweetheart, I've been looking all over town for you."

"Oh yeah?" I asked. He'd been looking for me?

Sam stepped back and Jack moved in close, pressing against me. I felt every hard inch of him, just as I had Sam when he first tugged me into the dead-end of the hallway. I had to tilt my head back to meet his eyes. "Yeah. If you want monkey sex, I'm the one for the job."

"Monkey—" I gasped, then pushed my finger against his chest, remembering what Elaine had written in her messages from the plane. "You read my instant message on my laptop!"

"Sweetheart, your friend wants you to get laid. To fuck a Montana cowboy. I'm the man for the job."

Sam cleared his throat. "We're the *men* for the job."

My mouth fell open, turned my head so I could stare at both of them. Both stunning examples of mankind. "You think I should just hop into bed... with both of you? I've never... I mean it's—"

Jack looked left, then right. "We're in the back hallway at a bar and you just had Sam eat your pussy. Good thing I was here to kiss away all those sounds you make because the entire bar would have known what you were up to otherwise. Besides, you seemed to be just fine with me joining the party."

I pursed my lips and gave him a glare I hoped would make him retreat.

"Whoa, now that's a look." Jack stepped back enough so I could take a deep breath.

Sam laughed. "Yeah, making her come was supposed to wind her down a little. Didn't seem to work. That death look, doll, doesn't work on him either. We know what you want. More orgasms. Hell, you *need* them. Let us give them to you."

"You know nothing about me," I countered.

"I know you taste like sugar and that you come like a dream." Sam lifted his right hand to his mouth, licked one finger, then another. "You're nice and sweet on my fingers."

My mouth fell open and I almost came right then. He did *not* just do that.

"Sweetness, I want you to ride me like you did on the plane," Jack said. "But in my bed and naked."

"Stop calling me that." I wasn't sure who I was mad at, them or me. It wasn't their fault I'd lost my head and did *that* with them. I was mad at myself for giving in to Sam's charms more than anything instead of stabbing him with my four-inch heel. Sure, he was hot. Sure, he knew *exactly* what to do with that tongue of his. That didn't mean I'd just give in, did it?

I stormed past them, down the hall and back into the main bar area, cut right on by and didn't look at anyone—definitely afraid that they'd know what I'd been up to—and out into the parking lot. The sun was just setting over the mountains and the air was softer. Cooler. It felt good on my heated skin.

"You're afraid," Jack called from behind me and I startled.

I shook my head and stared at the glorious sunset. All I could think about—ridiculous really—was why it wasn't dark at nine o'clock at night and not the fact that I'd just got it on with two men in the back of a bar. My mind was screaming "run, run" but my pussy was saying "more, more."

"I should have known you'd follow me," I said with a sigh.

"You think we'd let you walk to your car by yourself? I'm not sure what men are like in the big city, but here, a man takes care of his woman."

I spun on my high heels. "I can take care of myself." Crossing my arms over my chest, I dared them to disagree.

Sam walked slowly toward me. "I don't doubt that for a minute. But why would you want to?"

Jack moved to stand next to Sam. Some customers came out of the bar and walked to their car and I stayed quiet until their car doors closed.

"Because my vibrator doesn't prattle on like the two of you do."

Sam chuckled, took in my defiant stance. "God, I love a ball buster."

My cell rang and Sam pulled it from his pocket, looked at the screen.

I stepped forward and tried to get it from him. Yes, the asshole tossed it to his cousin.

I felt panicked at the sight of my phone, hearing it ring and not being able to answer it. "I need to get that."

Jack shook his head. "No, you don't."

"It might be Cara."

"It's not a Montana area code so whoever it is can wait."

"But it might be work."

"And it's nine, two hours later back east. They can fucking wait." Jack slipped it in his shirt pocket.

My mouth fell open staring as my phone disappeared.

"You know what she's doing?" he asked his cousin.

"Yup." Jack crossed his arms over his chest, mimicking me.

"What?" I asked, confused. The two of them individually were ruthless. Together, they were lethal. "What the hell am I doing besides trying to get my fucking phone back?" I tapped my shoe on the pavement.

Jack tsked me. "Language, sweetness."

"Bite me."

Jack looked me over as if debating where to do just that. My nipples were hardening as if letting me know they were volunteering.

"You're getting all angry so we'll make the decision for you," Sam said, pulling his keys from his pocket. A car chirped in the lot.

"You two could be axe murderers." I highly doubted it, but if they were, I imagined we'd fuck first, then they'd chop me up into bits.

Jack pulled out my cell from his pocket and fiddled with it. He put it up to his ear.

"What are you—?"

"Cara, hey, it's Jack Kane. Yeah, I've got Katie here with me. She'll be with us, so if you don't hear from her tomorrow, don't panic. She'll be sleeping off a night with the Kane boys."

He pushed the button on the phone, slipped it back in his pocket.

I couldn't help but laugh at the man's audacity, holding my phone hostage. And mortified. "Oh my God. You did *not* just say that."

Jack held out his hand. "Let's go, sweetness. We'll give you a night your friend Elaine won't believe."

What did he have, better than perfect vision, to see my IM so clearly? "Then I'll get my phone back?"

Sam laughed, slowly shaking his head. "We're not fucking you in exchange for your phone."

I arched a brow. If I gave in, would they think me easy? God, after what I did in the back hallway, the answer was definitely a yes. "Oh yeah?"

"We're fucking you because you need orgasms," Sam replied.

Jack nodded once, eyed me from head to toe. "Lots of them."

JACK

Bridgewater was small enough I figured I'd find Catherine either on my own or by enlisting help. I just didn't realize the help I'd be getting would be Sam's. And by eating her pussy. She wasn't just Airplane Girl either. She was little Katie Andrews, all grown up. I vaguely remembered her from... hell, fifteen years ago. She'd been all of twelve or so and had played with Declan MacDonald's kid sister. I'd been in high school at the time and a little kid wasn't even on my radar. I'd had my eyes on the cheerleaders. Hell, I'd been eyeing any girl with perky tits. I'd been a horny teenager and all I wanted to do was get my hands on some and get laid. I'd had a one-track mind back then.

Now, with Katie Andrews—all grown up—sitting between us in my truck, I still had a one-track mind. Her. I looked forward to getting my hands on her perky tits, too. I'd had a semi ever since they were in my face on the plane.

Just the sight of her as she was lost to her pleasure as she rode Sam's face had me almost coming in my pants. She was gorgeous all relaxed and flushed and while I didn't mind that Sam had made her that way, *I* wanted to put that look on her face. We should have gone to Sam's place since it was in town. Much closer to the bar. But I wanted her where she could be as loud as she fucking wanted; I didn't need one of his neighbors calling the police because Katie was a screamer when she came.

Since it was ten miles to the ranch, I needed to keep Katie's mind from turning back on. I remembered how she was on the plane, stressed and worried about work, overthinking. I had no doubt if she had her pilot's license she would have gotten her own fucking plane so she could be in control.

While I had her cell and she couldn't find out what was happening outside of the truck, she could simply turn on that Type-A mind of hers and start to analyze everything, to try to grab that control again. That was no fucking good. When she clasped her hands in her lap and started wringing them, I knew we were close to trouble. She needed to stay occupied and I knew just the way.

"Slip off your panties."

Her hands stilled and she looked up at me. "What?"

"Take off your panties," I repeated.

"Why?"

Sam shook his head and laughed.

"Because I want to see your pussy. I want to play with it on the way to the ranch. Because I want you thinking about what I'm going to do to you once we get there." *And nothing else.*

"We," Sam added. "What *we're* going to do to you."

"You had an up close and personal view of that pussy earlier. It's my fucking turn," I told Sam. I couldn't help the rough tone. She'd all but straddled my lap on the plane and *he'd* been the one to have her come all over his face. Not fucking fair. I could pound nails with my hard on. Just watching her, hearing her orgasm was almost enough to make me come in my pants. "Sweetness, take off those panties."

Even with her seat belt on, she was able to shimmy her hips and work the little scrap of lace down her legs and off. When she held them in her hands, I snatched them from her and stuffed them in my shirt pocket. I felt the dampness on them and her sweet scent rose up to me. *Fuck.*

"No more panties or I'll just keep taking them."

With one hand on the wheel, I placed the other on her thigh and worked her flirty little skirt up. Sam did the same with the other side and soon enough her pussy was exposed. Thank Christ for straight roads or we would have been in a ditch.

Only a hint of color remained in the sky, so only the lights from the dashboard illuminated her. I could see that she had a small triangle of hair at the top. Cupping her knee, I spread her legs apart. I ignored her gasp when I saw she was wet. Her little folds practically glowed with the pale blue light.

I couldn't resist and slid my fingers inward, sliding them over her. Wet and hot, like silk. As I parted her folds and slipped a finger inside of her, Sam found her clit.

When Katie rocked her hips up and a throaty cry filled the truck's cab, Sam said, "Stop driving like a fucking old lady. I want to come deep inside this hot pussy, not my pants."

I put my foot down on the accelerator. "No fucking kidding."

By the time I pulled up in front of the main house, Katie was on the brink of coming—her pussy walls were clenching my fingers— and she had a death grip on both our wrists.

"No coming, sweetness."

"What?" she cried, breathy and frustrated. Her dark gaze lifted to mine, confusion and passion warred.

"We're in charge now," I told her, so there was no question in her mind she wouldn't be running this show. "That includes your pleasure."

"We say how, we say when," Sam added, opening his door and hopping down.

After stepping out of the truck, I reached back in, slid her across the seat and threw her over my shoulder, ass in the air. Sam was ahead of us on the steps and I tossed him the keys.

"Jack! Put me down!"

Sam pushed the door open and I walked right through and up the stairs.

When she started hitting me with her little fists, I swatted her ass. "I'll put you down. In my bed."

"Jack!" she cried again.

"Spank her again. She likes it," Sam added.

At the top of the stairs, Katie stilled immediately and I gave my cousin a wide-eyed look. His only reply was a quick grin. Sliding my hand up her thigh, I lifted her skirt so it fell over her back, exposing a gorgeous ass. Pale and lush. I spanked one cheek, then the other.

She startled and cried my name again, this time with a little less anger and a lot more heat. Dipping my fingers over her pussy, I said, "You like it when your men take charge, don't you, Katie?"

I could feel her shake her head against my back. "No. You're crazy. I don't like being manhandled like this."

Sam turned on the lights and I dropped Katie onto my bed. She bounced once and she quickly scrambled up to her knees.

"You might be in charge in the courtroom, might run circles about men in your office with torts and depositions, but you need your men to take control in the bedroom."

I had no fucking idea what a tort was, stupid lawyer paperwork, but he was right about the rest. She needed to let go, to forget everything, to turn that smart mind off. If that meant spanking her ass and tying her wrists to the headboard, then that's what we'd do. "You can fight it, you can fight *us* all you want, sweetness, but your pussy never lies."

I grinned at her as I licked her wetness off my fingertips. Her eyes widened and her mouth fell open. Yeah, pure sweetness.

Beside me, Sam started to undo the buttons of his shirt as he toed off one shoe, then the other.

"Did you like the orgasm I gave you, Katie?" Sam asked, tugging his shirt tails from his pants.

She nodded her head, shifting her eyes to watch him undress.

"Good girl," I told her, relieved she wasn't going to get embarrassed now. "There's no shame in what you did. What we did. Here's how the night's going to go. We're going to get you naked, then we're going to fuck every last thought from your head besides my name and Sam's."

I gripped the front of my shirt and tugged, the snaps popping one by one.

"And if you start thinking again, we're going to spank your ass and then we're going to fuck you all over again."

"Ever been with two men before, doll?" Sam asked.

"No," she whispered.

"Then on your back and spread those thighs. Let's see that perfect pussy of yours."

Yeah, we were bossy. Yeah, she hated being told what to do, to give up her control to two men, based on the way her eyes narrowed in that *fuck you* stare she had. But she loved it, too, because she didn't say a word, only laid back on my bed, bent her knees and spread her feet nice and wide.

Not only did she have the most perfect pink pussy, but that little triangle of trimmed hair that pointed to the promised land proved she was a fucking natural blonde.

 ATHERINE

When Elaine said she wanted me to fuck a cowboy, she probably hadn't envisioned this. Me, with my legs parted, two cowboys standing big and tall before me, staring at my pussy. It was as if they were looking at the fucking Holy Grail.

"She's wearing too many clothes," Sam commented. He went to one side of the bed, Jack to the other and crawled on, slowly stripping me of my blouse, bra and skirt. I doubted I'd see my panties, the ones tucked into Jack's shirt on the floor, ever again.

"What about you?" While I was naked, they were still dressed.

It took seconds for them to strip bare and I couldn't decide which way I should look. On my right was Sam, my left Jack. God, two naked cowboys.

Sam was dark everywhere. He either tanned naked or was naturally dark-complected. He had a smattering of hair on his chest that tapered into a thin line beneath his navel and went directly to the thatch at the base of his cock. His very big, very erect cock.

Then there was Jack. Jack's hair on his head was fair, as if bleached by the sun. He, too, had hair on his chest, but it was darker than on his head. His cock was thicker than Sam's and a drop of pre-cum oozed from the tip. I wasn't sure if I could get that broad head inside my pussy, let alone my mouth.

I salivated at the idea of trying.

Perhaps he was a mind reader because he crooked a finger and I crawled across the bed toward him. I looked up at him through my lashes, his cock bobbing right in front of my face.

He gripped the base, stroked it once. "That's all for you. That pre-cum is for you. Lick it up."

His voice was dark and dominant and I knew that I was not in charge here. I was not in control. For the first time in... ever I was okay with that. I didn't need to think. I didn't need to worry about anything. We were going places tonight that I could only dream of, and then even further. I needed to let them guide me. If he wanted his cock in my mouth, that was fine with me.

As he held his cock for me, I licked the head like a lollipop, the sharp taste of his fluid coating my tongue. He groaned and it made me feel powerful. Opening wide, I took the head into my mouth. He was big. Holy hell, I couldn't take all of him. I'd heard of women taking a man's cock down her throat. That wasn't happening with Jack.

I felt the bed dip behind me and Sam's hand stroked down my spine. I sighed and closed my eyes at the decadent feel of it. A sharp swat to my ass had my eyes widening.

"Don't stop sucking Jack's cock, doll."

I pulled off him and looked over my shoulder at Sam. He grinned as he slid his hand from where he was caressing the spot he'd spanked and between my legs. "That look's going to get you fucked."

I didn't think it was possible to get any wetter, but I could feel it on my thighs, hear the sound of it as Sam's fingers continued to move. I shifted my hips, beginning to ride his fingers, but he spanked me again.

"Oh no, you don't. Suck Jack's cock, doll, and I'll give you what you need."

Looking up at Jack again, his eyes were hooded. He took my hand and wrapped my fingers around his cock. I felt it pulse beneath my palm, so thick, so silky soft yet hard.

"I shouldn't want this," I said. Was that my voice?

"But you do," Jack replied.

Flicking my tongue out, I licked off another pearly drop, let it coat my tongue. "But I do."

I took his cock as deep as he could go now, pumping my fist at the same time. I wasn't the best at this, but I had to hope my enthusiasm would mask any lack in skill. By the way Jack groaned, it seemed to be working.

Sam shifted on the bed. I heard a drawer open, then the crinkle of foil before his hand cupped my hip, held me in place as his cock slid through my wetness, pressed against my entrance, then slid deep in one slow stroke.

Fuck, the feel of him, stretching me wide and filling me so deep was incredible. I squirmed, unaccustomed to such penetration as I moaned around Jack's cock. The pleasure, hot and bright, made my skin tingle, my clit ache.

Jack's fingers tangled in my hair, guided me to take his cock as he liked.

Sam didn't move, held himself perfectly still as I closed my eyes and savored the thick feel of him. Of both of them. I was impaled front and back and I didn't want to be anywhere else.

"I'm not going to last," Jack said.

"Hell, I'm not even moving, doll, letting you adjust to me, and I'm going to blow. You've reduced us to horny teenagers."

I clenched down with my inner walls, feeling him, learning how he fit me. Sam groaned, spanked me again. I clenched even harder.

"Do you want to come, doll?" Sam asked, beginning to move his cock. In. Out. The pace was ridiculously slow, but every single nerve ending in my pussy was rubbed just right. His fingers gripped my hips, holding me just where he wanted me.

I couldn't do anything about it. Sure, I could tell them no and I knew they'd stop, but that wasn't what I really wanted. I wanted him to move *more*.

I couldn't nod as I sucked Jack's cock, so I made a sound, something close to a yes.

Jack groaned.

"Why is that?" Sam asked.

I pulled off Jack's cock and looked over my shoulder. "You want to have a conversation now?"

"Tell me why you should come."

"Fuck, Sam, I want my dick back in her mouth," Jack complained.

Sam's magical cock stroked over some place deep inside that had me arching my back and crying out. "There. Right there again. Please." I wasn't beyond begging. Not now.

Sam stilled. "Oh, no. Tell us why you should come, doll."

"Because...because I'm a good girl," I replied, breathless.

I was a total slut. What the hell was I doing with two men? One cock in my mouth, one in my pussy. What was I doing writhing and moaning, begging and *talking* about sex? Chad never went for any of this. Jack's hand covered mine on his cock and he began to stroke, slow at first, then harder and my ex was forgotten. Obviously, I'd been with a loser who didn't know how to use his cock because Sam was going to make me come and he wasn't even moving. Then Jack—

"Stick out your tongue," he said. I looked up at him through my lashes, saw the tenderness in his gaze that contrasted with the tense jaw, the corded muscles in his neck. His cock was right in front of my mouth, a dark plum color and shiny from my mouth.

It *was* naughty, but I wanted it. I wanted it all, so I did as Jack wanted.

Placing the tip of his cock on my tongue, he groaned. Thick pulses of his cum spurted into my open mouth and coated my tongue. I kept my eyes on his the whole time, reveling in the way his eyes closed tightly, his skin flushed. His lips formed a thin line. He exhaled deeply. I'd reduced him to sheer pleasure and he'd all but painted the proof of it on my taste buds.

When his cock had been emptied, he moved back.

"Show Sam."

Jack was a dirty talker. What he was having me do was so filthy, but all it did was make me wetter. I turned my head, looked over my shoulder.

Sam saw his cousin's seed in my mouth. "You're right. You are a good girl. Swallow, sweetness."

I closed my mouth and did just that. Jack's salty, tangy flavor coated my tongue and filled my belly. I'd never swallowed before, never enjoyed it, but with Jack, with Sam watching, I liked it.

Jack reached out, took my chin, tilted my head back so I had to look at him. With his thumb, he brushed off an errant drop of cum from the corner of my mouth. "Open."

I did and he slipped the tip of his cock back in.

"Clean me up." I licked the flared head clean. There was no missing the pleasure in his gaze or the way his cock was still hard.

Sam leaned over me, placed his hand beside mine on the bed. His warm body pressed against my back, the soft hair of his chest tickling my sensitized skin.

"I changed my mind. You're not a good girl. You're very, very naughty," he murmured. "You've just swallowed Jack's cum while my cock fills your tight little pussy. You think you should come?"

"Yes!" I cried.

He licked the shell of my ear, tsked me. "You get to come because you like to suck cock. You like to take two men at once." He swatted my ass, the hot sting of it making me gasp, especially when it only made me ache more, made my clit pulse. "You like to be spanked."

"Yes!" I repeated. I did.

Scooping me up, Sam pulled me upright so I was straddling his thighs, our knees bent. I was sitting in his lap with his cock embedded deep. He held me in place with his hands on my breasts, Jack right in front of me.

"Jack's going to watch you come."

Putting one knee on the bed, Jack shook his head. "Not just watch. I'm going to help."

He reached between my legs and flicked my swollen, sensitive clit.

"Oh!" I cried, trying to shift my hips. I couldn't, Sam's hold too tight. Sweat coated my skin. The scent of sex swirled around us, dark and carnal. This wasn't like anything I'd ever... *ever* done before.

Sam began to lift and lower me as he thrust his hips up, fucking me now. His time for holding still had passed. His drive toward coming was fierce and he took me hard, pinching and tugging on my nipples as he did so.

With his mouth on my neck, Sam groaned, I felt him thicken and lengthen inside me just before he came. I was right there with him, so hot, so needy, so ready to give over to my own pleasure, but I couldn't do it. I couldn't get there, even as I tried to shift my hips. I cried out with equal parts need and frustration.

"Katie," Jack said.

I opened my eyes, looked up at him, whimpered.

"Come now."

He pinched my clit. Hard. I should have hated it, should have been stunned he'd done something so painful. Turned out, it wasn't painful at all. Or it was the most exquisitely painful pleasure I'd ever felt and I came. I screamed, my body milking Sam's cock, trying to pull him impossibly deeper into me.

He panted as his pleasure waned, holding himself so far into me surely Jack could feel him against his palm on my belly.

Jack took me in his arms as Sam pulled out, tugging another whimper from me. Jack tucked me in beside him on the bed, my cheek resting on his chest, one arm over his waist. Sam had gone to the en suite bathroom to dispose of the condom, but returned quickly and moved to lay behind me. I was still between them and I felt... well used, well fucked. Protected.

My eyes were too heavy to open, my body too replete to do more than idly swirl my fingers through the hair on Jack's chest. I couldn't even think of any reason why what we'd just done was a bad idea. I knew the thoughts would eventually surface, but not now.

Sam kissed my shoulder. "Sleep, doll. You're going to need it."

$\mathcal{S}$AM

As I expected, when the sun came up, so did every one of Katie's walls. Jack, used to getting up at the butt crack of dawn, was in the kitchen when Katie stumbled down for coffee. I'd woken when she had, and soon followed. I felt loose and relaxed in a way I hadn't felt in a long while. A way that only several orgasms could achieve. Jack had the same shit eating grin that I knew I wore.

How Katie was walking properly, especially in those sky-high heels, was beyond me. After I fucked her the first time, we took a little break before she woke up to Jack's head buried between her thighs. We'd taken her a few very creative ways—except at the same time—until she passed out with exhaustion.

"Coffee," she muttered, standing beside the coffeemaker waiting for Jack to pour her a cup. She grabbed onto the mug like a lifeline and breathed in the rich scent before taking her first sip.

"Do you need—"

She held up her hand, cutting me off, as she stared at the steam coming off her drink. "No talking until I have coffee."

I nodded slowly, then took the mug that Jack handed me. He grinned and we watched Katie drink her coffee, all rumpled and looking well fucked.

It should have been an awkward silence, but either Katie's brain didn't turn on until after coffee—something to remember—or she wasn't the least bothered by tag teaming two men last night. When she put her empty mug on the counter a few minutes later, it seemed it was a little of both.

"I guess I'm not getting my panties back?" she asked Jack, her voice that stern librarian tone again.

Shit. My cock thickened in my pants realizing she wasn't wearing anything beneath that cute skirt.

Jack grinned and slowly shook his head. "Nope. And, like I said last night, if you wear them around us, we'll keep taking them."

Her mouth fell open, but she quickly shut it. Narrowed her eyes. *There* was the look. God, I loved that look. All ball withering and in complete control. I wanted to take her right back upstairs and make that go away. Nah, I could just bend her over the kitchen table.

"And my phone? If I see either of you again, will I be handing that over, too?"

"Not if. *When.*" Jack crossed his arms over his chest and didn't smile. "Sweetness, we might control you in the bedroom, but there's no way in fucking hell we want to control your life. I couldn't juggle that many balls if I were in the circus."

She opened her mouth to speak, but Jack shut her down. "But, if it's after business hours and you're working your tail off, then the answer's hell yes, we'll take your phone."

Katie held out her hand and practically tapped her foot on the kitchen floor waiting.

Jack pulled the phone from his shirt pocket—he was the only

one of us wearing fresh clothes since we were in his house—and handed it to her.

Spinning on her heel, she walked out of the kitchen with her head down, her fingers flying over the screen. Her heels clicked on the wood floors to the front door as she started talking to herself.

I looked to Jack and he just smiled and shook his head once more. "She talks to herself when she's stressed."

"There's no service here!" she called, her voice angry and panicked at the same time. "I can't check my email. No texts. No voicemail messages. It's after nine in New York. Do you have any idea—"

"Woman," I shouted, putting my mug on the granite counter. "Chill the fuck out and I'll get you back to civilization."

"Keys to the truck are by the door. Tonight?" Jack asked before I walked out.

I grinned. "Winding her down is going to be a nightly occurrence."

———

"Are we going to pretend last night never happened?" I asked.

I'd taken her back to her rental car in the bar's parking lot and ensured she sped off in the direction of her uncle's house before I turned toward the office. Three hours later as she sat across from me at my desk, she didn't have that mussed up, I-just-had-sex look about her. Which was terrible. I liked it much better than her hair pulled back neatly in a ponytail—one which I'd love to grab hold of as I fucked her from behind... again—and another prim blouse and skirt. Her heels were gone and in their place a pair of purple flats. I'd never seen shoes that color in Montana before.

She lifted her head from the papers before her to look at me. "I'm reading legal documents. Do you want me to pant over them?"

My eyebrows went up, then couldn't help but grin. "That would certainly make it better."

She rolled her eyes and got back to reading. While her cell was on the desk in front of her, she'd set it to silent when she sat down, knowing that while this wasn't her job, it was why she'd flown across two time zones. She was in lawyer mode. I respected her focus, but wished she took the same principle to task in her personal life, putting value to it.

"They're standard forms. The quit claim deed transfers the property to you today. If we get them signed before noon—" I stressed this as she was taking a damn long time to go over them. "—the courthouse can file them before the end of day."

"You want *me* to chill the fuck out," she mumbled, shaking her head and picking up the pen. With a flourish, she signed at all the designated spots and slid the pile over to me.

"I was where you are, you know," I told her, lifting the papers and tapping the bottom of them on the desk so they all lined up before stuffing them in a yellow envelope. "I left Bridgewater when I was eighteen, went to college, then law school on the west coast. I went corporate, just like you. Did the whole eighty hours a week deal, the partner track. No life. Just worked my ass off for three years. Cell phones, email, texting, IM, deadlines, heartburn pills, I know all of it."

I had her attention. "Why did you come back here then?"

"Because one of my dads had a heart attack. A small one, and he's fine now. But I came back for about a month to help out and realized I didn't need to live with the insanity. It was sucking the life from me, so I walked."

"Didn't you want to make partner?" she wondered.

I shrugged. "That was what drove me for so long, like a carrot dangled in front of my face, then realized I didn't really want it. It was time to come home to my family."

"Yeah, well, my parents aren't a ray of sunshine." I waited, hoping she'd add to that. "They're thrilled I'm a lawyer because they're lawyers. They think this time before partner is called paying my dues." She lifted her hands and made those curled finger air quotes.

"Why don't you go into practice with them?"

She laughed. "I'm guessing your family had dinner every night together. You do Sunday dinners, spend Christmas wearing ugly sweaters, right?"

I nodded. "The ugly sweaters only come out for the holiday party, not on the actual day itself," I clarified.

She, too, nodded slowly. "My parents are retired and travel. I see them about twice a year for lunch when they are in the city to switch out their clothes in their luggage from summer- to winter-wear. Last Christmas they were in Hong Kong. I ate a frozen dinner while watching football on TV. And I worked."

"Of course," I added. Of course, she worked on Christmas. Fuck. The idea of her being alone in New York while I was with my parents and cousins, aunts and uncles was a sucker punch to the gut.

"We aren't huggers or Sunday dinner people." She sighed, sat back in her chair. I didn't see any sadness about her, just resignation. She was resigned to having shitty parents, to being alone. "Besides the two meals a year, I get a phone call when my mother hears about an update to the Law Journal. We're not much of a family."

It was obvious to me now. She kept herself busy enough so she wouldn't realize how fucked up her life was. If she slowed down, she'd realize her parents were assholes and her job sucked. So she just kept juggling all those fucking balls.

"Family isn't always defined by blood. You can make your own family. I came back here to start one of my own."

She stiffened and color drained from her face. "You have a wife?"

I shook my head, ran my hand over the back of my neck. "Jesus, Katie. Of course not. Before you ask, neither does Jack. But if we're going to share a wife, it helps to be in the same town."

Her mouth fell open. "You want to...to share a wife?"

"Yes." I told her the truth and succinctly. There was zero question she could misconstrue that answer.

She frowned. "Um... last night, yeah. That was a one night stand."

"Get laid by a cowboy... or two, right? Get it out of your system."

"Well, yeah. That's what Jack said at the bar."

I stood, went around the desk so I was right in front of her. She had to tilt her head back to meet my gaze. Leaning forward, I put my hands on the arms of the chair, caging her in. I picked up her scent. Lemon. Tart and sweet, just like her. "So I shouldn't feel any chemistry between us? I shouldn't want to press you over my desk right now and fuck you."

She flicked her gaze at my desk, then back to me. Licked her lips.

"This is the twenty-first century. You don't have to marry me if we have a one night stand."

Taking her ponytail, I slowly wrapped it around my hand, anchoring her in place. "What we're doing with you, this isn't a one night stand, doll. I know it. Jack knows it. You know it, too."

When I gave the silky strands a little tug, she whimpered. I saw the flare of heat in her pale eyes, the memory that we were in charge.

"Was last night enough?" I had to know.

"No," she whispered.

That one little word had my cock go instantly rock hard as relief swept through me.

"You're wet, aren't you? I bet you've been wet since you left our bed."

She swallowed. "Yes."

I groaned, then bent down and kissed her. Her mouth opened and my tongue instantly tangled with hers.

I could drown in her, drown in the knowledge I held her head as I wanted so I could claim her mouth. She would think of nothing but my lips on hers, my tongue tangling with hers because of the tight hold I had on her hair. I was in charge and she reveled in it.

I lifted my head, released my grip. Stepping back, I pointed to my desk.

"Bend over."

I'd give her soft words and gentle caresses if I knew that's what she wanted. Those weren't for her. She wasn't that kind of woman. She wanted to rule her own little world, but she wanted me and Jack to rule *her*.

"Here? Now?"

"The cool thing about my job is that I can fuck you, right here. Right now."

She stood slowly, but while her cheeks were flushed and her eyes glazed with lust, her damn mind was getting in the way and she was thinking again. "What about Jack?"

"I don't need him to fuck you."

"But... isn't it cheating?"

"It's cheating if you fuck Kara's brother, Dec, instead of one of us." When she didn't seem satisfied with that answer, I grabbed my phone, dialed Jack. "Hey. Hang on," I told him, then passed Katie the phone. "Here. Tell him your problem."

Her eyes widened. "My problem?"

Hitting the speaker button, I grabbed the phone back, set it in the cradle.

"Katie's here with me in the office."

"Hi, sweetness," Jack said through the speaker. "What's your problem?"

She flushed a bright pink, but didn't say anything.

"Her pussy's wet," I said.

She gasped, grabbed her purse and laptop bag, ready to flee. Grabbing her about the waist, I held her securely as I put her two bags back on the floor.

"That is a problem. Isn't Sam taking care of that for you?" Jack asked.

"I am going to kill you," Katie said through gritted teeth, trying to fight my hold.

"Ah, there's my girl." I loved it when she was all riled. I had a challenge before me, to fuck that anger right out of her. "She's worried you'll be mad. Right, doll?"

"If you have needs, sweetness, if you're pussy's all wet and needy for a cock, then you can tell one of us. We'll take care of you, I promise. If I'm not around, it's Sam's job to tend to you."

With one arm banded about her, I used my free hand to unbutton her blouse. A lacy pink bra appeared, almost too delicate to handle the hefty load of her full breasts. I didn't have to dip my fingers beneath the fabric far to find her soft nipple. She gasped.

"If I'm not around, Jack will fuck you," I murmured, kissing her right behind her ear.

"That's right," Jack confirmed. "Why's your pussy all wet, sweetness? Does it miss our cocks?"

I pulled on her nipple then, tugging it then releasing.

"Sam," she gasped.

I studied her profile, the bright flush in her cheeks, the way her eyes fell closed and she bit her lip. She liked nipple play and I wasn't going to stop. Sure, I'd stop if she wasn't into it, if she told me no, but the way she moaned, the way she arched her back into my touch, that was the last word she was going to utter besides "Yes," and "Please," and "Harder."

"Answer his question, doll. Do you miss our cocks?"

"Yes!" she cried, when I pinched the hard tip.

My hips shifted into her lower back, my cock already hard.

"Then let Sam fuck you. He'll make it all better." Thankfully, Jack was on board with what she needed.

Katie whimpered when I released her tight little tip.

"Are you wearing panties, sweetness?" Jack's question had her stilling.

I laughed. "Uh oh. I think she is, cousin," I said aloud, dropping my hand from her waist. "Hands on the desk, doll. Let's see if you're a bad girl."

She took a deep breath, then another before putting her hands on my desk.

"Bend those elbows and stick that ass out."

Those dark eyes met mine and held as she did as she was told. Stepping behind her, I slid her skirt up her thighs, exposing every creamy inch, and her white silk—barely there—panties.

"Christ," I muttered, seeing the delicate fabric soaked through with her arousal.

"Panties?" Jack asked.

"Yup," I replied.

"Take them off, sweetness."

Using one hand at a time, I watched as she worked them off one hip then the other before they slid down her legs.

"Leave them around your ankles," I said. The sight of her, skirt up, pussy dripping and exposed as she bent over my desk had my pants tenting. I had to adjust myself to ease the ache in my balls.

I went around my desk, lifted my briefcase on top and pulled out the condom, lube and plug I'd tucked into a side pocket, placed them in front of her. Her eyes widened as she knew what they were for, but she didn't move, didn't do more than squirm.

"What...what are you going to do with those?" she asked, her eyes focused on them.

"We took you last night, one at a time. When you have two

men making you come, you'll have one fuck your pussy, the other your ass. This plug will prepare your ass to take a cock."

"Last night was a one-time thing," she countered as I went around behind her.

"And yet, here you are, bent over my desk, pussy out with your panties about your ankles."

"Sam, I—" she said, but Jack cut off whatever she was going to say.

"Sweetness, we might take charge when it comes to fucking, but you have all the power." His voice came through loud and clear from the speaker. "Just pull up your panties and tug down that skirt. You can say no. It won't hurt our feelings none. We'll just court you proper until you're ready."

He paused and she didn't move.

"Or, you can take that plug, take your punishment and take a good hard fucking."

She lifted up on her palms. "The plug is punishment?"

With a hand on her back, I pressed her down to her elbows, then reached around to grab the plug and lube.

"Hell no. The plug's for your pleasure."

"I don't think something in my ass is going to make me feel good."

"Ever tried it?"

She shook her head.

"Never had that ass fucked?" Jack asked, since he couldn't see her little head shake.

"No," she said.

Jack's growl came through loud and clear.

"Get that ass prepared, Sam."

She startled at the sound of the lube's lid opening. With a few drops on my fingers, I slid them over her folds, then settled on her crinkled—and virgin—asshole.

"Shh, doll. Only pleasure."

79

Her body stiffened as I circled my finger, so very gently. I continued until she relaxed, until she began to wiggle her hips. I doubted she even knew she was doing it. Only then did I apply a touch of pressure. Placing the little bottle above, I squeezed a few more drops and then pressed inward.

"Sam!" she cried and I was sure Jack could hear her ragged breathing.

"Do you know what I'm doing over here, sweetness?" Jack asked.

I slid in and out, but only to the first knuckle, adding more and more lube. I wanted her to be super slick before I put the small plug in, knowing it would slide in nice and easy.

"I'm standing in the tack room stroking my cock. Just knowing how you're taking Sam's finger has my balls drawn up."

Katie whimpered and dropped her head down onto her forearms.

I took that as a sign and pulled out, quickly coated the plug and pressed it against her. "Deep breath, doll. That's it, let it out nice and slow."

As she did, I slipped that plug right in, her passage so slick and ready. When it was seated, I gave it a gentle tug and her head came up, my name a shout on her lips. I couldn't help the grin.

"Like that? You should see it, Jack. The plug is in perfectly. The little jeweled end is all pink and sparkly."

It was a decorative plug, a pink faux gem in the wide flange.

"Just as pink as her pussy?" Jack asked.

"Yup, and in just a minute, just as pink as her ass. Ready for your punishment, doll?"

She looked over her shoulder at me. "Punishment? But..." She sputtered when I stroked my hand over her upturned butt cheek, then gave it a little swat.

"No panties," Jack said.

"But you only said you'd take them away."

"It's just a reason to spank you," I said, giving her another swat and watching as my handprint bloomed as pink as her plug. "We learned last night how much you like it."

"I do not," she sputtered.

"Then why are you still over my desk? Why are you pushing your ass out for more?" I spanked her again, nice and easy. We were overwhelming her enough. But she sure as fuck wasn't thinking about anything but us right now.

She stilled then and she whimpered once more, realizing I was right.

I spanked her five more times, the last so I nudged the gem handled plug.

"Good girl. You should see how beautiful she is, Jack."

She was. So hot, so sweet, so submissive. Perfect.

"You'll have to show me later, sweetness, how pretty you look with that plug in your ass. Now I want to listen to you come. I'm going to come all over my hand when you do."

With gentle fingers, I slipped through her dripping folds, slid into her pussy. She pushed back, fucking herself. "Want to come, Katie?"

"Yes!"

"With my fingers or my cock?"

"Your cock, please."

As I undid my pants, grabbed the condom off the desk and slipped it on in record time. If she wanted my cock, I wasn't going to deny her.

Gripping a hip, I aligned myself to her slick entrance and slid in. With the plug, it was a tight fit, but she was so wet for me I filled her in one long stroke.

"Oh god," she groaned.

When my hips were pressed against her heated ass, I leaned down over her. We were completely dressed except for the important parts. It was the most erotic fuck of my life and I doubted I'd ever get any work done at this desk ever again.

"Feel good, doll?"

She nodded her head.

"How's it feel to be fucked with a plug in your ass?" Jack asked. "Imagine what it'll be like when that's my cock instead? Sam in your pussy and me taking you there. Both of us."

His words had me close to coming. I wanted to fuck her with my cousin, to claim her completely. Make her ours.

"Yes," she whispered.

I took her then, deep strokes, slow at first, watching her face, seeing her pleasure in her profile. When I was sure she could handle more, I fucked harder, deeper. Rougher.

"This is so dirty," she said, her voice rough with her need.

With one hand pressed into the desk, I reached around and found her clit, all hard and swollen for me.

"Time to come, doll. Come for me. Come for Jack who's listening on the phone."

She did, on command, and wasn't quiet about it. Her inner walls clenched down like a fist, so tight and hard that I couldn't hold back.

"Fuck," I growled as I plunged deep one last time, lost in her, the pleasure of the orgasm. It stole my mind, my cum as it filled the condom, making me wish the latex barrier wasn't between us. I wanted to take her bare, to coat her with cum and mark her as mine. But it wasn't my right yet. Soon, but not until she belonged to us.

I heard Jack grunt through the phone, knew he, too, came.

Gripping the base of the condom, I carefully pulled out as Katie lay slumped on the desk, her breathing ragged, her eyes closed.

"Later, Jack," I said, hitting the button on the phone to disconnect. "Come on, doll. We've got to meet the Realtor." After wrapping the used condom in a tissue and tossing it in the trash, I fixed myself, zipping up my pants and tucking in my shirt.

Slumped over the desk, she looked so mussed, so well fucked. I was getting hard again just looking at her. Slowly, she came up onto her elbows, her breasts thrusting enticingly over her bra and out from her blouse's opening as she caught her breath. "What?"

"You want to sell the house, don't you?" I glanced at my watch. "I thought you'd like my quick pace, being from back east and all. We were supposed to meet her about ten minutes ago."

She stood abruptly then, her mind already working. Well, not completely since she stood there with a plug in her ass, her skirt about her waist and her panties around her ankles. "Are you serious? We did... *that* while you knew we had a meeting with the Realtor?"

I grinned. "Damn right. Sally won't mind. Want me to take that plug out or do you want to leave it in?"

She stiffened then, remembered herself. Glancing over her shoulder, she flushed a bright pink. Fuck, she looked good in pink. All over.

"Here, let me help." I fixed her bra, then her blouse. Turning her about, I carefully pulled the plug from her, grabbed a tissue and set it on the desk. Grabbing another tissue, I reached between her legs to clean her up. She swatted my hands away.

"I can do that."

"I know you can, doll, but it's my job to take care of you. If I made you messy, then I need to clean you up."

When her eyes couldn't meet mine, I kissed her forehead. Tossing the tissue in the trash, I watched as she reached down to tug up her panties.

"Oh no. Those belong to me now." I held out my hand and watched as various emotions flit across her face. Surprise, embarrassment, menace. I didn't say a word, just waited. It was a battle of wills and when she huffed, I knew I'd won. At least this fight.

She pursed her lips and stared daggers at me.

"Want another spanking? I know how much you'll like it. But then we'd be even later."

That stirred her into action, lifting one foot then the other and dropping the minuscule panties in my open palm, then working her skirt down her hips. "She's going to know what we did."

"By the just fucked look on your face? Absolutely."

I could have sworn she growled at me, stomped out of the office and slammed the door on the tiny powder room. When I heard the water running, I had to laugh as I tucked her panties in my pocket. Fuck, she was perfect.

When she came out a minute later, she was all set to rights, although she did have that soft, sated glow about her. Hell, I knew I had a shit eating grin of a well fucked man.

"Isn't she going to be mad waiting for us?"

"You're one of those who hates to be late, aren't you?" When she just gave me the death stare, I added, holding my hands up in front of me, "Sally has lunch at the same time and the same place every weekday."

Besides being a good Realtor, Sally Martin was also motherly, a ball buster and knew everything about anything going on in town. Including my actions, and probably quite a bit about Katie. She'd also been married for forty years to the mayor and a town vet. While Cara might be able to talk to Katie about being married to two men, she was in that honeymoon stage which was almost syrupy sweet to watch. Sally's marriage was the real deal and had made it the long haul. It was something I wanted Katie to see, to realize that being with two men wasn't just a one night stand, but could endure.

With every button she'd done up, her walls went up again. It was almost a tangible thing and I couldn't help but grin.

"She's going to know," she repeated.

I took in her flushed cheeks, her red lips, her tousled hair. Anyone looking at her would know she just got fucked, and well. I didn't think it was a good thing to say anything more if I wanted to keep my balls, so I just took her hand and tugged her out of my office and down the street.

10

ATHERINE

Sam did a really good job of fucking my thoughts right out of my head. As he led me down Main Street I realized he'd mentioned sharing a wife with Jack. Not sharing *me*. A wife. When a man used that word... ever, it's a big deal. No guy ever tossed it out there, especially if it pertained to them. But Sam was so casual about it, as if he really wanted a wife to share his life with—and his cousin.

What we were doing together wasn't a big deal. Sure, I'd never had a threesome before, never had a guy fuck me over his desk either while his cousin listened in on speaker phone. Never had a bejeweled plug in my ass. None of this bossy shit that seemed to make me ruin my panties—before I was forced to hand them over.

For me, it was a big deal on the 'ways I've had sex' scale, but it was casual. Fine, it wasn't a one night stand. It was a short term, week-long fuck fest. I was going to go back to New York with my orgasm quota checked off for the year. That was it. I didn't have time for anything else. I didn't *want* anything else. Did I?

Jack and Sam were nothing like Chad. They were gentlemen, albeit horny ones. They held doors, made sure I was safe, even made sure I came first, even if that involved a finger or a plug in my ass. God, I could feel the remnants of that play as we walked down the street.

The chemistry was off the charts, that whole butt play proving it, and... well, they were just nice guys. Hot, horny, dominant, nice guys. They made me think about things I never considered before. Living in Montana, two men, hell, a whole new life. No. My life was in New York in that corner office, not between them in bed. I pushed those thoughts to the back of my mind and focused on getting Charlie's house sold.

Turned out, Swan's Diner was only a block away from Sam's office. It sat on the corner of Main and Hogan, where the only stoplight in town—in the county, probably—was situated. The building, like all others, was old and brick. The interior didn't have the polish The Barking Dog did. Like Charlie's house, it hadn't been updated since the seventies. The booths were red, the counters white with gold sparkle in them. There was even a jukebox in the corner. Smells of coffee and grilled onions were strong when we entered and Sam steered me toward the back. It took a few minutes to get to Sally's table since Sam had to shake hands and say hello to everyone on the way. He knew *everyone* and he'd made introductions, although they all knew me, whether by the gossip mill or remembering me from when I was kid visiting Charlie. There was Bob, the man who ran the feed store. Miss Mary, Sam's pre-school teacher—yes, she had to be ninety-seven. Karl, the long-haul trucker.

They'd all been really nice, which had been a shock. As Sam talked highway construction with Karl, I realized there was something really kind of wrong with me if I was shocked people were nice. Nice! What had I expected? I expected them to know that I'd somehow bent over Sam's desk and let him do stuff to me that was probably illegal in Utah and Alabama. I expected them to know I had no panties on.

If they somehow knew—perhaps because of the very satisfied look on Sam's face—they didn't mention it. They were nice. There was that dang word again. People weren't all jackasses in New York, but everyone had a game plan, an agenda. A mental to-do list that didn't include asking after their mother or finding out if their pumpkins were going to be in the State Fair again this summer. Crap, I just described myself.

This feeling of community, of caring, it was odd. It was... nice. Damn.

As we headed toward the back, Sam froze. "Shit," he whispered.

"What?" I asked, looking around. Nothing seemed out of the ordinary other than me stepping into Happy Land.

"Brace yourself. You're strong. You can handle it." Sam didn't say more, but guided me toward the back booth with a hand at the small of my back.

Dread filled me—for what, I had no idea—but his hand seemed less courteous and more of a preventative measure to keep me from running away.

"Mom," Sam said.

Oh shit. She would know what we did and think I corrupted him with my slutty, big city ways. Not just her son, but her Jack as well. I'd just let Sam fuck me over his desk while his cousin listened through the speaker phone.

A woman in her early sixties stood and faced Sam, smiled. While he gave her a very warm hug, she smiled at me over his shoulder. She didn't look surprised at all by our arrival.

Of course. *I* was the reason she was here, not to see Sam. If she lived in town, I had no doubt they saw each other all the time. She wasn't missing him, she didn't want to miss seeing me. What had everyone been saying? I inwardly cringed at what this woman was going to do? Stab me with a butter knife?

I was right, I was her sole focus, because she nudged Sam out of the way to get to me. It wasn't hard to do, for while she was a foot shorter, she was sturdy and I was sure she'd run roughshod over him a time or two. She had short dark hair, gray strands attractively threaded throughout, and a quick smile.

"I'm Violet, Sam's mother and Jack's aunt."

I held out my hand—it was definitely sweaty and I wiped it on my skirt first—and she shook it, but then pulled me in for a hug, my arms trapped at my sides. "Honey, we hug everyone around here."

She was warm and soft and smelled of flowers. Her embrace was heartfelt and it was nice. I couldn't remember the last time—or ever—my mother hugged me. And yet I was a stranger to this woman and she pulled me right on in. Were people crazy here, or was it me?

"How did you know where to find us?" Sam asked.

Violet waved her hand. "Katie's in town to deal with Charlie's estate. She met with you to get the legal paperwork signed and of course she'll want to sell the house. Selling the house means meeting Sally Martin and Sally Martin always eats lunch at the same time and the same place. It was simple logic."

"Of course, it was," Sam murmured, the corner of his mouth tipping up. He offered me a quick glance, but said nothing. What could he say besides *run*?

"Sit...sit, or we'll never eat," Sally commanded. "You know how my blood sugar gets." The blond woman at the table had to be Sally. Where Violet was all baked cookies and flower gardens, Sally was all dual wheel pickup truck and hunting rifles.

Violet didn't even blink at the other woman's sass, but sat back down and slid into the booth across from her friend. Sam gestured for me to sit beside Sally and when I did, he took the place next to his mom.

"Heard you two had a date last night."

I flushed red and Sam thanked the waitress for his glass of water. Either he'd had enough one night stands to be unaffected by such questions or he was a natural at faking it. "If you two know everything, why are we even meeting?" he asked.

If she knew *everything,* I'd be run out of town.

"Well, it's been awhile since you and Jack had a woman together," Violet said.

I almost choked on my spit.

"Mom, that sounds completely inappropriate," Sam scolded, completely unfazed by his mother.

"I didn't mean it that way," Violet replied, then glanced to me. "It's been over ten years since you two were interested in a woman together. Your fathers and I are pleased. For you, and Jack."

"Fathers?" I asked, looking at Sam. "You have two dads, too?" God, he had said *one* of his dads had had a heart attack, but I hadn't processed it. It was just so dang weird.

"Oh yes, dear," Violet answered for him. "I married Tom and Harris Kane almost forty years ago."

"I was a bridesmaid," Sally said. "Fortunately, bridesmaid dresses were pretty back then. What colors are you thinking?"

I realized both women were staring at me and my deer-in-headlights look.

"For what?"

"Don't scare her," Sam warned. "Seriously. She's a lawyer in New York and is only here to—"

"We know all that, son," Violet said, patting his shoulder. "We'll let off on the bridesmaid dress colors if you come to dinner at the house before you leave."

I looked between Sally and Violet, slowly shaking my head. "Wow, you guys are good. You played your own son. Nice," I applauded. "I either have to listen to you plan my wedding to Sam and Jack or come to dinner. How can I refuse such an arm twisting invitation?"

I narrowed my eyes at Sam, but he was probably smart to flag down the waitress.

Sam's mother was no idiot. Neither was Sally, but I wasn't marrying her son. I'd have to keep an eye on both of them. While Sam and Jack could talk me out of my pants—and my panties, those two could have me down the aisle. Or worse.

"So you want to sell the house?" Sally seemed to know when to change the topic of conversation.

I pulled a straw from the wrapper, stuck it in my water. "It needs tons of work. The bathroom is the color of an avocado and there's a rooster clock on the wall in the kitchen. It's like stepping back in time and while I think vintage is cool, this is like the Brady Bunch meets Montana."

"I remember that rooster clock," Violet said, amused. "I'm amazed it still works."

"That property's value is in the land and the water rights," Sally told me.

The waitress stopped by, pen and paper in hand. "Usual?" she asked.

I glanced at the others, who all nodded.

"Um, are there menus?" I wondered. I didn't see any propped up by the salt and pepper shakers against the wall.

Sally patted my hand. "We come here enough, honey, that we don't need them. Jessie knows everyone's orders by heart. I'd go with the cheeseburger if I were you."

"Not a salad?" I asked, thinking how many calories were in a burger.

"You're not one of those veggie types, are you?" She looked aghast.

"No." I picked up my water, took a sip. "Just watching my weight."

Sally eyed me. She shook her head. "Cheeseburger."

I glanced up at the waitress who was already writing that down. "Gotcha."

It seemed I was having a cheeseburger.

"Can you explain to me about water rights?" I asked.

Sally nodded, waved to someone across the room, then turned to me.

"While the State of Montana owns all waters within the state on everyone's behalf, if a body of water flows through your property, you get the rights to use the water. There are senior water rights and junior water rights. The property with the oldest priority date has the more senior right to the water. Meaning, that property gets 'first dibs.' If someone with junior rights is redirecting the water of a more senior right, they can force the junior person to stop or change."

"It sounds like Kindergarten," I replied.

Sally nodded shrewdly. "It is, but there's no real sharing. If you've got a senior water right, you can redirect for livestock, a creek diversion, crops, whatever. It's a big deal out here."

"So Charlie's water rights are senior?"

Sally laughed again, deep and throaty. "Honey, *your* water rights are the oldest in the county. I think they date back to the 1880's. Part of the original Bridgewater ranch. Meaning you can practically do with that creek of yours whatever you want." She held up a finger. "Almost."

Sounded complicated and pretty interesting. "It's an interesting study for a lawyer."

"It's a big deal for Realtors, too. You're familiar with reading dry and boring things in your profession, so this should be right up your alley."

"Because of these water rights, the property is even more valuable then."

Sam turned his hand from side to side. "The water rights themselves are valuable. You, as the property owner, can sell the water rights alone to someone and keep the property. Or the reverse. You can sell the property and hold on to the water rights."

"I'll have to check it out. It just seems strange that Charlie would leave it all to me. I haven't seen him since I was twelve."

Violet looked thoughtful. "He knew the reason why you stopped coming."

I frowned. "Well, I don't."

Violet's eyes widened. "You don't?"

"My parents said they had a falling out. That's it. After that last summer, we just never came back."

"Well, he cared for you and I think he thought the place would be good for you."

The waitress brought our orders, balancing them up her arms. My cheeseburger was enormous and the pile of fries beside it had enough carbs to make me diabetic. I thought about Violet's words as everyone started to eat. Why did he think the house would be good for me? Right now, it was only adding to my stress. If I sold it, I'd have a nice nest egg. If I kept it, I could come here in the summers, but the upkeep would be costly, and I couldn't look at that rooster clock forever.

"If you really want to sell, the house will need to be cleaned out before it goes on the market."

I nodded. "I figured. I think Charlie kept every paper and plastic bag he ever got from the grocery store and he has a hobo figurine collection that scares the crap out of me."

Violet laughed, pointed her fork at me. "I remember those. They are creepy."

"I can meet you at the house tomorrow morning. Sound good?"

I cut my burger in half, lifted the bun and poured ketchup on it. Glancing quickly at Sam, I saw him grin around his own burger. The man had plans for me tonight, special plans that could potentially keep me from another meeting with Sally.

I narrowed my eyes at him. "Sure. What time?"

11

ATHERINE

I'd been at the coffee shop for two hours. The woman who ran the place, Maude, knew who I was and greeted me by name. She didn't mind that I'd taken over a table in the corner near a plug where I could charge my laptop and my phone. She didn't mind that I was using her for her internet connection, especially since I was on my third mocha latte.

While I was slogging through my emails, text messages, voicemails and IM's, my mind wasn't completely focused. I was a little sore from a wild night with the Kane boys and then the steamy follow up with Sam in his office. It didn't help that the chairs were hard, and I found myself squirming a fair amount. Damn them for distracting me—and the spanking!

It wasn't just the ache and throb of my body, but my mind kept wandering to the feel of them, all soft skin over corded muscles. Their voices, rough and almost arrogant in their need. The scent of them, spicy cologne and musky sex. The orgasms. Yes, I was the screamer Jack had pointed out.

I'd never screamed when I came before. Then again, I'd never been taken by anyone who knew what they were doing before either. I'd thought Chad had skill, but no. He had no clue where any of my hot buttons were. Sam and Jack did. Every. Single. One.

Frowning down at my laptop, I tried to force myself to concentrate. I'd never get anything done if I kept getting distracted by memories of the Kanes and their deliciously clever moves.

"Katie?" a decidedly chipper voice called from the front of the coffee shop.

Looking up from my screen I caught sight of a petite young woman with long brown curls heading my way with a wide, welcoming smile. The two leashed puppies trailing behind her attempted to sniff and hump every piece of furniture in their path but eventually they reached my side and I found myself face to face with Little Mary Sunshine. I didn't think I'd ever met someone so intrinsically... happy.

"You must be Katie," she said, shoving a hand in my direction, not seeming to notice that her dogs were going wild licking my new, pricey flats like I'd just waded through a puddle of bacon fat.

"Hi," I said, trying to match her level of enthusiasm and failing. Was I supposed to know her from when I was a kid?

"I'm Angie," she said. "Cara's best friend. She told me all about you."

Oh, did she? For one brief, paranoid moment I wondered what Cara had said. Was *everyone* in this town aware that I was in the middle of a Kane boys' sex sandwich? Did people know what we did in the bar hallway?

"She said you inherited your uncle's place?" she asked. "Real nice man—I sure hope you're going to stay."

I blinked a couple of times at her rapid pace, unsure of what I was supposed to respond to first. "Yes, he was a great guy." *From what I remember.* I felt so bad not knowing more, remembering more, about the man who seemed to have thought so highly of me. "As for the house, I haven't decided yet what I'm going to do with it."

And that was the truth—from what Sally said, I'd need to do my research before I made any decisions. As for her comment about whether I was going to stay... hopefully I managed to sidestep that nicely.

Of course I wouldn't stay. I couldn't. I had a job to get back to. A career. One I worked my ass off for, thank you very much. It wasn't like I could just walk away from that just because there happened to be two sensational lovers in Montana who knew how I liked it, even better than I did. An unbidden image of Jack's cock in my mouth as Sam fucked me from behind rose up in my mind and suddenly oxygen was in short supply.

Oh shit, the coffee shop was way too warm. Didn't they have AC?

If Angie noticed my sudden discomfort, she didn't let on. She was too busy prattling on about the countless charms of Bridgewater. Either this woman worked for the tourism board or she really did want me to move here.

Why? Maybe it was the jaded New Yorker in me, but I couldn't imagine why Angie—or Sally or Cara or anyone else for that matter—cared where the hell I ended up. They barely knew me but they were more invested in my future happiness than most of my acquaintances back home. Heck, no one would have come up to me, a stranger, in a coffee shop unless I'd stolen their seat.

But, other than Elaine, no one would care if I disappeared off the face of Manhattan. Life would go on as usual with or without me. I had to wonder how long it would take before my parents realized I wasn't even in town. God, those were depressing thoughts.

"Okay, well, I better get these pups off their leashes before they go nuts," Angie said, that broad smile never faltering. "Will I see you at Cara's tonight?"

"Um..."

"She should be calling you soon with the details," Angie added. Apparently this woman knew my social calendar better than I did.

"I hope you can make it," she added. "I'll be there and so will Declan."

As if on cue, my phone vibrated and Cara's name popped up on the screen. I held it up to show Angie. "Speak of the devil."

She grinned—of course she did—and started to back away, mouthing the words "see you later" even though I hadn't answered the phone yet.

Sure enough, Cara was calling to invite me to dinner. "Jack and Sam Kane will be there," she added, her voice filled with laughter. Yup, it was official. My threesome was public knowledge.

I would have said yes anyway but the fact that they would be there definitely added to the appeal. Why did my heart skip a beat at the mention of their names? The now-familiar ache between my thighs intensified as if on command. Good Lord, I hadn't known the Kanes for more than twenty-four hours and I was already hooked on them like a drug.

No, not them. I was hooked on amazing sex. A woman could become addicted to multiple orgasms from two hot cowboys if she wasn't careful. And it wasn't just orgasms. It was dirty, rough, wild sex. With orgasms.

After hanging up with Cara, I turned my attention back to work. Or I tried, anyway.

The phone rang again and I didn't look at the screen, thinking it was Cara again.

"Did you sign the papers?"

Chad.

All my good feelings slipped away.

"Leave me alone, Chad." I sighed.

"That property is half mine."

"Talk to my lawyer."

His bark of laughter had me wincing. "What, you can't represent yourself?"

I could, but then I'd have to listen to his shit.

"Talk to my lawyer," I repeated.

"And who would that be?"

Sam's smiling face came unbidden to my mind. I wasn't going to subject him to Chad, though. I wasn't that cruel. "If you figured out about my uncle's land, then you'll figure this out, too."

I disconnected and sighed, taking my mug to the counter for another refill.

After returning to my seat, I tried to get my head back in the game. While Sam and Jack made my mind go blank, Chad had the ability to make me obsess about how stupid it had been to have married him. Dwelling on it only gave me heartburn, but I couldn't help it. He was such a prick and I'd been stupid. Naive. No longer.

I was finally able to focus, but I didn't make much progress before my attention was diverted once again—this time by an IM from Elaine that popped up on the bottom of my screen.

How's the monkey sex?

My snort of laughter made me choke on my coffee. Slapping a hand over my mouth to stifle it, I looked around guiltily. The last thing I needed was someone else reading my personal messages.

I stared at the message screen debating my response. Elaine was clearly teasing with her monkey sex comment—she hadn't seriously expected that I would have a one-night-stand with a cowboy any more than I had. But if she only knew....

Oh, what the hell? If there was anyone who wouldn't judge—who would applaud, even—it was Elaine. And Cara. And Angie.

Probably Declan, too. Sally. Even Violet. So I typed the words, hit enter.

I did it.

I bit my lip to hold back a ridiculously girly giggle. But really, it wasn't every day I could tell my best friend that I'd had a threesome. With two cowboys. Two insanely hot, drool worthy cowboys.

Her response was instant. *You did not.*

Elaine, you had no idea.

I did, I swear.

Elaine's response was a series of exclamation points and question marks. Clearly my friend was too excited for words. I drew in a deep breath before taking the plunge.

You're not going to believe this, but...

I hesitated for one second. It was one thing to have a fling with a pair of cowboys, twice... so far, but it was quite another to admit it. Somehow telling Elaine made it real in a whole new way. It was one thing if everyone in Bridgewater assumed, it was another to own up to it.

It wasn't like I was ashamed, just... shocked. By myself—by how much I liked it. Up until yesterday I never would have considered that I might be into a threesome, let alone a polyamorous relationship. Let alone doing butt stuff.

Not that this *was* a relationship. It was just sexy times... with butt stuff.

What the fuck, Catherine! Are you trying to kill me with suspense? Who did you do? And more importantly—how was it?!

I grinned at the screen and quickly typed my response. *Two cowboys. HOT cowboys. And it was epic.*

Elaine's response came two seconds later. I assume she needed that time to digest this bit of news. Then I got: *WOOHOO!!!!*

From her spot behind the counter, Maude glanced over with a smile at my choked laugh.

We went back and forth for a while as Elaine demanded *all* the details. I'm pretty sure she was trying to live vicariously through me, and I couldn't say that I blamed her. Her consensus? *Keep fucking the hotties as long as you can.*

This, according to Elaine, was my once in a lifetime opportunity. And maybe she was right. It couldn't last forever but I could enjoy the hell out of it while it lasted. Hell, I could make enough memories to last me a lifetime with my vibrator once I was back in the real world.

My stomach sank at that bleak image of my future—cold, passionless. Lonely. But it was the life I'd always known and I'd be fine once I was back in my element. Back in the bustling city, back to my full schedule. The meetings, the long hours. Somehow that reassurance didn't quite ease the hollow feeling in my chest, but I chose to ignore it.

Speaking of the real world... I couldn't put it off much longer.

What's going on at work?

There was a pause before Elaine typed, *Are you sure you want to know?*

That alone was enough to make my blood pressure rise and the acid in my stomach churn. Did I want to hear about all the shit going down at work? No, not really. I had an idea, but I had to know the truth, so I told her to spill. I almost wished I hadn't when Elaine's rapid-fire one line texts popped up on my screen, each one worse than the last.

Seemed Roberts was still on the Marsden case and telling everyone it was his—no big surprise there—but he'd also weaseled his way onto another one of my cases.

Fuckity fuck. Fuck.

I'd asked Farber about that case in one of my emails and he'd never responded. Guess now I knew why—he was too chicken shit to outright tell me he'd screwed me over. Again. The worst part was, I wasn't all that surprised. Pissed, definitely, but I couldn't pretend like I hadn't seen this coming. Farber and Roberts were two peas in a pod with their little golf outings and their squash games. I'd known from day one that my firm was an old boys' club, but I'd hoped that my hard work and dedication could break through all that crap. And I'd only been gone two days.

My hands were shaking with anger, making it hard to type. This wouldn't have happened if I hadn't left. I hadn't taken a day off since being hired, even going in when I had the damn flu last year. Then I leave for two days! I gave those two assholes the opening they'd needed to squeeze me out. Elaine must have known exactly what I was thinking.

They're pulling the same shit they did with Margaret Stern.

The air rushed out of my lungs. She was right. This was exactly like Margaret Stern, a former employee who'd been on the partner track when I started at the firm. Elaine and I watched from the sidelines as she got screwed at every turn by Farber and his cronies. After a couple of years of being shafted, Margaret resigned and we all knew it was because they'd forced her out.

Stupid me, I'd watched that happen but I still thought that I had a chance, that maybe I would be different. If I worked hard enough and played by their rules, I could earn the role of partner. Yeah, right.

As if the system wasn't rigged against me from the start just because I had a vagina. As if Roberts hadn't been the favorite all along.

I shook my head with disgust at my personal pity party. Wallowing in anger at the unfairness of it all wasn't going to get me my case back and it sure as hell wouldn't win me the partner position. Neither would remaining in Bridgewater County, Montana. I needed to make sure Roberts and Farber knew that I wouldn't let them walk all over me. If I wanted to claim what was mine, I had to get back to New York and take it back.

12

ACK

Katie was standing in front of the coffee shop when I pulled up in my truck. Sam walked toward her from the opposite direction, apparently coming straight from his office. He spotted me and gave me a small nod before we both turned our attention to Katie, who hadn't glanced up from her phone long enough to see us coming. We'd texted to tell her we would pick her up to take her to dinner at Cara's once she finished up her work, but from the looks of it, our girl still hadn't called it quits for the day.

Of course, she hadn't. I wouldn't expect anything less from our little workaholic. But I still had hope that we could tempt her away from the rat race and into our lives...for good.

That death glare she aimed at her phone was goddamn adorable, if you asked me, but it was frustrating as hell to see her all worked up over that crappy job of hers. Sam reached her side first and his voice was surprisingly gentle. "Put it away, doll. Work time is over."

She looked up at him and blinked as if just now realizing where she was and why. She turned those big baby blues in my direction and it was all I could do not to scoop her into my arms and kiss her until she forgot all about the damn phone. Her work. Hell, New York City. Better yet, haul her into my truck and fuck her brains out until she was too blissed out to care.

But as quickly as she'd looked up, she turned her attention back to that fucking phone. "Hang on one sec. I just have to send one more email."

Sam arched his eyebrows at me over the top of her head. *Just one more email.* Our Katie sounded like a damn junkie when it came to her work. There would always be one more email. I knew this because Sam had been just like this. Until he saw the light.

I was ready to snatch the phone out of her hand right then and there but judging by the understanding look on Sam's face, he knew exactly where she was coming from. Being a former workaholic himself, I let him take the lead.

"What's the emergency this time, doll? Tell us about it."

Huh. This was a new tactic. I trusted my cousin and it seemed his approach was exactly what she needed because Katie's shoulders slumped with something that looked heartbreakingly like relief at having a sympathetic ear. Snatching the phone would only mean we didn't understand, which was probably true, at least for me. I'd always wanted to run the ranch. No rat race for me. Hell, the only rush hour traffic I ever saw was when a herd of cattle stopped traffic as it crossed the road.

"It's that asshole Roberts," she muttered as she stabbed at the keypad of her phone. "He took my case and he's trying to steal another. And Farber is letting him!"

She glanced up at us and I swear her eyes were wild with a frantic energy. A mix of stress and anger that had her wound up so tight, she could snap at any second. Now, I had no idea who Roberts and Farber were but I would beat the shit out of them on the spot just for putting that look in her eyes.

"Then there's my ex. He keeps calling and he sent an email to mess with me."

I could see Sam felt the same way judging by the tightness around his mouth and eyes. Ex? He hid his anger better than I did, but either one of us would put our lives on the line for this woman —and kill for her, if it came to that.

Her ex was fucking with her? He was a dead man and we had hundreds of acres to bury the body.

"He's already junior partner and gloating," Katie continued. I wasn't sure if she was talking about Roberts, Farber or her ex. Her fingers were still flying over her phone and though she might have been standing in Bridgewater, her mind was clearly thousands of miles away.

"Would that be so bad?"

We both shot Sam a look of surprise at that. Katie, for obvious reasons, but for me—I could see where he was going with this. I just hadn't expected him to bring up this conversation quite so early in the night, or while Katie was in one of her stressed out stupors, for that matter. I'd kind of envisioned this talk happening when all three of us were naked and content in bed.

But hell, if Sam thought it was time, I was game.

"Would that be so bad?" Katie repeated the question slowly as if it was the most ludicrous thing she'd ever heard. "Of course, it would be bad, Sam. I've worked my ass off to make partner. I've earned it."

"No one's saying you don't deserve it." I tried to keep my voice low and soft, the way I'd talk to a spooked horse to make sure it didn't hurt itself or me. Sure enough, she swung around toward me with those wide, crazed eyes.

I cocked my head, studied her. "Sweetness, just how many coffees have you had today?"

She ignored the question as she turned back to Sam. "How can you ask that?" she insisted. "You of all people should know how hard I've worked for this... how much it means to me."

Sam took a step closer and placed his hands on her shoulders. From where I stood, I could see the gravity written all over his face and knew Katie had to see it, too. "I'm sorry, Katie. Real sorry. I know you've worked hard, and there's no doubt that you've earned that promotion, but is that what you really want?"

He might as well have been speaking Greek. Her brows drew together as she turned from him to me in confusion. "This is what I've been working for forever. Of course, this is what I want."

"You really want to work for some douchebag chauvinist pigs?" I asked, taking a step closer so I could reach for her hand and soften the blow. A real man might be dominant, commanding and very demanding, but only to protect his woman. Not to fuck her over. "Do you really want to work your ass off for a firm that doesn't value you?"

Tugging her hand out of my grip, she backed away from me. From us. "What is this about?"

Sam gave me a questioning look, and at my nod, he spoke. "We want you to stay, doll."

And there it was. My cousin had just spelled it out for her and now our future was on the line. There was a tense silence as we watched her closely. Watched as she shook her head.

"I've already stayed here too long. I need to get back to New York before Roberts—"

"He means, for good," I added, though I figured she knew that. "With us."

Judging by her skittishness, she was well aware we were talking about more than just extending this fling by a day or two. She instantly defaulted to anger, like I knew she would.

"You can't possibly expect me to drop everything—my career, my home, my friends. I have a life, you know."

"And I'm sure it's a good one," I lied. What she had back in New York was no life—it was a rat race. An endless competition where the winner got an ulcer and a heart attack as a prize. And an ex who seemed to like to fuck with her. I caught her gaze and held it. "But we'd like to think you could have an even better life here in Bridgewater... with us."

Sam stepped in, coming closer to her other side so she was surrounded by her men, forced to listen to us. "We want you with us for the long haul, doll. You're the one for us."

Scoffing, she crossed her arms in front of her chest. I had to assume she wasn't aware that she'd just made her tits jut out in spectacular fashion. Of course, that made me hard, but now was not the time. I had to will the fucker down.

"You can't possibly know that I'm the one. It's too soon, too—"

"We know," I said. My tone left no room for argument, but that didn't stop her from trying.

She gaped up at me. "We've only been together—if that's what you want to call it—for one night. And... and whatever that was on Sam's desk. You can't possibly be sure—"

"We *know*, doll." Sam looked at me to explain.

I gave Katie a shrug. "It's the Bridgewater way. When two men find their woman, they just know. It's like lightning—"

"Oh, please," Katie interrupted, clearly not buying it. "Declan gave me that whole 'lightning strike' speech. Do you really expect me to believe it's that simple?"

Sam's voice was low and gruff, filled with more emotion than I'd ever heard. "Do you really expect us to believe that you don't feel it, too? That when we touch you, it isn't... more?"

Her stunned silence was answer enough. For the first time since we arrived, some of the tension eased out of my shoulders. She felt it, she just didn't want to admit it. I hadn't even realized how nervous I'd been to have this talk—cowboys weren't exactly anxious by nature—but this was a big fucking deal. Her response would affect the rest of our lives.

She seemed to know it, too. For the first time since I met her she seemed at a loss for words.

Sam took her by the elbow and steered her toward the truck. "Come on, doll, we've got a dinner to get to."

It wasn't until we were all in the truck that Katie came back to her senses. "You can't seriously expect me to give up everything and move to Bridgewater."

"Look at you," I said. "You're so stressed out over this job, you can barely see straight. Is this really how you want to live?"

She glared over at me. "That's easy for you to say. You haven't spent your entire adult life working toward a career goal. It's not that easy to walk away from."

I shrugged. She had a point. I had the ranch, but I wouldn't say there was any need to move up any damn corporate ladder. Sam was the career-driven one in our family. He caught my look over her head and by silent agreement we let the conversation drop. There was no point in arguing with Katie—she could out-argue both of us, if we let that quick brain of hers make all the decisions. No, if we wanted to win her over we'd have to show her what she wanted. Let her body and heart decide.

"Hand over the phone, doll." Sam held out his hand and when she hesitated, he lowered his voice in that commanding way of his. "We're done fighting with you, Katie. You know the rules."

She passed him her phone but not without a grumbled protest. "God, I'm surrounded by bossy men."

"Sam and I are nothing like those assholes you're working with."

"We're just looking out for you, doll." Sam placed a hand on her thigh and her breath hitched. I'd bet money that pretty pussy of hers was already wet from that simple touch. "And I want you to tell us all about this ex of yours."

She sighed.

"Now, sweetness," I added. Had he hit her? What the hell was this asshole doing to her?

In two minutes, she offered a succinct outline of her ex-husband's pestering. It was that and that alone.

"He has nothing. No legal grounds," Sam said.

"I know. He just wants to mess with me."

"You'll give me his number and I'll take care of this. Of him," he added.

"What? No, I can take care of it myself."

"Of course, you can," I cut in. "But let Sam help. You're not alone anymore. You don't have to take care of everything."

She looked to me, then Sam.

"All right."

I was surprised, yet thrilled she'd given in so easily. If we could get her ex to leave her alone, then that was a damn ball she didn't have to juggle.

"Your priorities are out of whack," I told her as I squeezed her thigh, slid my hand higher. "It's up to me and Sam here to help you sort out what's important in life."

"And I suppose sex with you two is the most important thing." Katie's tone was sharp but I saw the way her chest moved as she fought for air. She wasn't unaffected, no matter what she said. Like we told her, her body never lied. Oh yeah, she wanted us just as much as we wanted her.

"Not just sex," Sam said. "This isn't about sex. It's about what's between us. We want you to be happy. Satisfied. You deserve to be treated right and taken care of every day of your life, not just when you're visiting Montana on family business. We're the men to do that."

Turning the ignition, I glanced over at Katie's lap. "Pull up that skirt for me, sweetness. I need to make sure you're not wearing any panties."

She shifted in her spot next to me. "I'm not. Sam took them from me this morning when we, um…"

"When he spanked and plugged that perfect ass then fucked you?" I finished. I loved the way her cheeks turned red. But even better was the way she fidgeted on the bench between us, a sure sign her pussy was throbbing, just aching to be filled. I hadn't fucked her yet, only had that sweet suck of her mouth on me and I was dying to be balls deep.

My cock was hard just thinking of the sounds she'd made back in Sam's office. I'd come all over my hand and onto the dirt floor of the tack room just listening to them. Hearing her beg for her pleasure, scream her release. Hell, there was no way I'd make it all the way back to the ranch. Heading toward Sam's place which was right in town, I tugged at the hem of her skirt. "Show me."

"I told you, Sam took them," she snapped.

God, she was feisty when she was horny.

"Show him," Sam commanded.

Slowly, teasingly, she pulled her skirt up the rest of the way so her pussy was exposed and I groaned at the sight. Sure enough, she was wet. I couldn't resist. Reaching out, I stroked her wet folds, slipping two fingers inside her tight pussy and made her moan. She wriggled her hips a bit and I knew she wanted more. She wanted me to finger fuck her and stroke that clit, but there was no way I was letting her off that easy. Nor was I doing it while I was driving because when she came on my fingers I'd surely drive us right into a ditch. And, a quick release in the car wasn't what I wanted for her. Our Katie needed to be shown just how badly she needed this—needed us.

I shot Sam a look and he helped me hold her hips still so she was pinned in place on my hand. With a quick glance over I could see her biting her lip to keep from moaning again. Maybe even keeping herself from begging for more, especially since I was holding my fingers still, just reveling in the way her muscles rippled and clenched around them.

"Isn't Cara's house the other way?" she said, her voice high-pitched and breathy.

Dammit, I'd forgotten all about Cara's dinner. I slid my fingers out of her pussy and licked them clean as Sam deftly took my place, his fingers thrusting into her roughly and not moving, just like I'd done. When she arched her hips and tried to fuck his fingers for release, he chided her softly. "Sit still, doll. We'll take care of you when we get home, I promise."

I reached for my phone and called Cara, told her we'd be running a little late. Judging by Cara's laughter, she could guess why.

Katie was quiet the rest of the way to Sam's and that was just fine by me. Hopefully, she was thinking over what we'd said. Maybe if we gave her some time, she'd realize we were right. And if that didn't work, I planned on showing her just how good it felt to be loved by the Kane boys.

Sam acted quickly the moment the truck came to a stop. In one move he got out and pulled Katie out after him, slinging her over his shoulder and hauling her into the house, ignoring her protests at being tossed around like a sack of potatoes.

By the time I followed them inside, Sam had already ordered Katie to bend over and put her hands on the kitchen table. Sam was clearly distracted at the sight of those gorgeous breasts straining against her shirt as she bent over. As he worked to free them from the straight-laced button-down top and frilly bra, I came over and gave him a hand by pulling up her skirt to reveal that full, luscious ass.

She gasped with outrage when I nudged her legs apart, but didn't try to stop us. Our little Katie needed another spanking and she knew it. What better way to get her mind off that crazy job?

I stepped back and watched as Sam smacked her ass once, twice.

"Again?"

"Again," Sam said, the sound of the slap echoed off the tiles. "When you stop thinking about work, we'll stop spanking you." He did it once more and I was mesmerized the way her creamy flesh shifted beneath his palm. "Well, maybe not."

My cock had been hard as a rock in the truck and I was just about ready to explode watching that ass turn red and those tits sway at the impact. But that was nothing compared to the look on her face—the exquisite mix of pleasure and pain that had her biting her lip and arching her back, silently begging for more. Yeah, she wasn't thinking about work now.

A few more slaps and all three of us were ready to come. I saw Sam fumble with the button of his jeans as he got ready to fuck her from behind. She was primed and ready—but I could make it even better. Dropping to my knees behind her, I parted those sweet cheeks and saw her wet and waiting. That was all the invitation I needed.

Her thighs stiffened beneath my hands as my tongue found her pussy. Wrapping one arm around her hips, I flicked her clit as my tongue laved her from behind. Her moan was low and sweet as I heard a condom wrapper open.

Now she was ready. I'd no sooner pulled back when Sam pushed me out of the way and shoved his cock into her in one hard thrust that had her gripping the edge of the table and calling out his name, my name—hell, the woman was screaming for both of us and God, too.

I came to her side and licked her ear, nibbled at her neck, pinched her nipples while Sam fucked her hard. All the while I whispered in her ear how fucking hot she was. How naughty. I told her that she was ours and only ours. I didn't stop until she was screaming that, too. That she was ours.

She and Sam came quickly.

"About damn time," I muttered, grabbing a condom of my own, opening my pants and sliding it on. "You've fucked her three times now and I've yet to be in that pussy."

It was finally my turn. Scooping her limp body into my arms, I headed for the couch in the living room, leaving Sam to clean himself up. Hair tousled and damp with sweat, that damned skirt that was still cinched around her waist, Katie had never looked more fuckable. I could hardly wait for my turn, but first I had to make sure she knew who was in charge.

I set us both down on the couch and then pulled her so she was sprawled facedown across my lap. Her rounded bottom still bore some red marks from the spanking Sam gave her but nothing that wouldn't fade within the hour.

"Jack!"

"My turn, sweetness. My turn to prove you belong to us."

"By spanking me, too?"

"You love it. And it makes you focus on just me. My hand, my cock pressing into your belly. My control."

I gave her a few light swats, then a little harder, making her yelp.

Now, I had to do my part to show her how good it could be if she let us take care of her. If she chose us for her husbands, we would be in charge and she would love it. I told her that in some form or another as I brought my hand down on her ass.

"Tell me what you want, sweetness."

She raised her head slightly, just enough so I could hear her say it. "More."

"That's right, sweetness, you'll never get enough of us taking care of you."

I brought my hand down again and then rubbed the sore flesh, soothing the sting I knew she felt, knew only made her hotter. I heard Sam mutter, "Oh holy fuck" when he entered the room. The sight of Katie sprawled across my lap with her ass in the air had us both horny as hell.

He sat beside me on the sofa, positioning himself so his cock—already hard again—was under Katie's head. No one had to tell her what to do next—she took the length of him in her mouth and let Sam guide her head up and down in time with her spanking.

I waited until I couldn't last any longer, the sight of Katie sucking on Sam's cock as she got spanked was just too damn hot. In one motion, I repositioned us so she was on all fours, her head in Sam's lap and her ass in the air.

She never stopped sucking on Sam, not even when I slid my cock inside her pussy and started fucking her. I couldn't help the groan that tore from my throat. She was so hot, so tight. So wet. When I teased her asshole, her moans were muffled by his cock. Sam came first and I watched our girl swallow as he arched his hips up off the couch. She followed close behind, a pinch of her clit sending her over the edge and taking me with her. I couldn't hold back, my need to come too great.

She was perfect. Just what Sam and I had been hoping for in a woman. She wanted both of us equally. Saw us both as two individuals, but jointly as the men who could give her the focus she needed and the sweet orgasms she deserved.

It wasn't until we were all cleaned up and sprawled across the couch that the topic of her staying came up again. Katie's head rested against Sam's chest, her legs in my lap, looking content and happy, and just a little smug with that shit-eating grin of hers and that made me feel like a cave man. Yeah, our girl had all the damn power.

I smoothed a hand over her thigh. "Do you believe us now, sweetness?"

Katie's eyes were soft, sated—a far cry from the stressed, crazed look she'd been wearing when we first picked her up. "Do I believe what?"

"That we want you for the long haul," I said, giving her thigh a squeeze. "That you're ours."

Surprise flickered across her face but she hid it with a smirk. "Was that the message I was supposed to get from what just went on here?" She waved a hand toward the kitchen table where she'd been fucked senseless. "Because honestly, I don't see how spanking me so much gets that across."

Sam tweaked her nipple through her opened blouse, making her squeal with surprise and pleasure. "We spank you because you're ours. Because you deserve to have two men looking out for you and making sure you've got your priorities straight."

She was quiet, which was a rare event in and of itself. I took that silence to be a good sign. At least she wasn't fighting us on the idea.

"We'll keep showing you just how much you mean to us," I promised. "Even if that entails a spanking, sweetness. It will be our pleasure to show you what it could be like if you stayed... but we can't make you leave your life in New York. That's up to you."

She looked down at her hands, which were intertwined with Sam's, but she still didn't respond. Sam gave me a small, encouraging smile over her head, but tension made it strained. This was it—we were laying it all out on the line for this woman. A first for us, and definitely our last. We'd been raised to believe that when we met the right woman, we'd know.

We sure as hell knew when it came to Katie—but there was no guarantee that she would feel the same way.

13

ATHERINE

Sally stood next to me in Charlie's living room and we surveyed the remarkable myriad of trinkets, knickknacks, and souvenirs that covered every available surface. I was exhausted just thinking about how long it would take to clear it all out.

"That is some creepy shit," Sally said, looking over the top edge of her glasses. She was staring at the hobo figurine collection that lined a bookcase shelf.

I nodded. It truly was.

Sally walked the length of the room, taking it all in. "So, how was your dinner at Cara's last night?"

I didn't even bother to ask how she knew about that. I was starting to resign myself to the fact that there was no such thing as privacy in a town the size of Bridgewater. "If you get a colonoscopy, does everyone know?"

She just eyed me like she had the figurines until I answered her question. Clearly, she knew diversion when she heard it. Fine. "It was nice."

Nice. As if that covered it. Dinner at Cara's had been eye-opening, but there was no way I could explain that to Sally. How could I tell someone who'd lived in Bridgewater her whole life just how incredible it was to witness such a joyful relationship. Cara and her husbands were so content. So... happy. The men doted on Cara, and she clearly reveled in it. She was the center of their world and it showed in every gesture. Just as the Kane boys were trying to tell me it would be like with them. Again and again, and it seemed when I was bending over a table or their strong thighs and getting spanked.

Is that how it would be if I married them? Not spanked, but doted on? It wasn't even a question, really. Last night I'd gotten a taste of what it would be like to truly be with them—to be their woman. I'd experienced hot sex with Sam and Jack, but I also got a glimpse of what life would be like outside of the bedroom.

They'd been attentive and thoughtful just like Cara's men were toward her. For the first time in my life, I'd been the most important person in the world to somebody. To two somebodies. I'd been the center of their attention, even in a roomful of people.

After dinner we'd gone back to Sam's place and they'd made good on their promise to keep showing me how it could be. Oh fuck, it could be *so* good. I'd had more orgasms than I'd thought possible in one night. And when we'd fallen asleep I'd been surrounded by my men, my head resting on Sam's chest while Jack's arm wrapped around my waist. When I woke up in the middle of the night, I'd felt safe in a way I hadn't since I was a little girl.

More than that, I'd felt... whole. Complete.

"Judging by that smile you're wearing, I'm going to guess you had a *very* nice night." Sally's laughter brought me back to the present and I feigned a sudden interest in Charlie's collection of movie ticket stubs to avoid the topic. I picked one up and examined it. "Was Charlie sentimental or just a hoarder?"

Sally eyed me and offered a soft smile. "You don't remember much about Charlie, do you?"

I shook my head. I'd been trying to call up specific memories of my summers here with my uncle ever since I'd arrived in Bridgewater, but all I could recall when it came to Charlie was a general feeling. I remembered a large man who'd pick me up whenever I cried—a man who was comforting to be around. Comforting, but sad. Though why he was sad, I never knew and was too young to think too much of it.

"He was a good man," Sally said.

"That's what people keep telling me." Something had been nagging at me since I'd arrived and when I looked around now, I realized what it was. There were no pictures. For a man who held on to sentimental knickknacks and hideous hobo figurines, it seemed odd that there were no pictures of family. He was a man who clearly loved Bridgewater and its ways, so why didn't he have a wife and husband? Even though it felt awkward to be asking a near stranger about my family, I had to know. "Did my uncle ever have a Bridgewater relationship?"

Sally looked over in surprise, putting down a stack of National Geographic magazines she'd moved. "You don't know?"

I shook my head. "My mother doesn't talk much about her family, and she never mentioned Charlie after she cut ties with him."

Sally sighed and crossed her arms over her chest, leaning against an end table. "Charlie was married. He and his best friend met the woman of their dreams right out of high school. They were quite the threesome—always did everything together."

I tried not to let my shock show. Maybe I should have guessed, but it was impossible to imagine someone from my uptight, straitlaced family living an unconventional lifestyle. My mother definitely didn't.

"So, what happened? To his family, I mean."

Sally's face fell, her mouth tightening into a thin line. "Car accident."

The two words made my heart ache on Charlie's behalf.

"It happened, oh, some thirty years ago," Sally continued. "Such a tragedy. Poor Charlie never truly recovered."

Suddenly this odd assortment of memorabilia and little treasures wasn't funny, it was tragic. Charlie had gone from having it all—the kind of happiness I'd witnessed between Cara and her husbands—to nothing. Not even his sister and niece. Me. I was an asshole for not knowing, for never asking. Granted, I'd been a kid when my mother said we weren't returning to Bridgewater to visit anymore, but I'd been a grown up for quite a while now. Why hadn't I thought to ask about him or, better yet, reach out to him myself?

"I can't believe my mom never told me," I said. "I can't believe she turned her back on him after he lost everything."

Sally shrugged matter-of-factly. "I remember your mother. She was in my sister's class in high school. As soon as she graduated, she was out of here." She snapped her fingers.

I nodded. That much I'd heard from my mother. On the rare occasions that she mentioned her childhood in Bridgewater, she was always quick to add that she'd escaped this Podunk town as soon as she was legally able. Knowing what I knew now, her sudden departure took on a whole new meaning. She hadn't left because the town was small or backwards or even ridiculously conservative, which was a complete joke. She'd left because she didn't like the way Bridgewater people fell in love.

A new thought had me staring open-mouthed at Sally. "Did my... I mean, were my... oh shit, were my grandparents polyamorous?"

Sally let out a sharp bark of laughter. "They sure were."

They'd died when I was young and I didn't really remember them, but with this new information, pieces of a puzzle clicked into place. "So my Great Uncle Albert—"

"Was your grandfather."

Holy. Shit.

"They were happy, too," Sally added. "A solid team, a role model for younger people like myself and my husbands."

"I can't believe my mom never told me."

Sally gave my arm a little pat and I realized then that I was staring into space with my mouth still hanging open.

"Even though she grew up here, I don't think your mother was ever comfortable with the Bridgewater way."

All I could think of was *duh.*

Sally moved past me toward the kitchen. "If you ask me, that's why she stopped coming here."

I looked over at her in confusion. "Why? Why stop coming to visit entirely and all of a sudden? Charlie was a nice man, from what I remember. Everyone I've met this week has said so."

"He was, honey." Sally stopped in the doorway to the kitchen. "But your mother... While she may not have been comfortable with the Bridgewater way... I think she realized that you *were.*"

I held up a mug with a picture of South Dakota's Corn Palace, frozen. "I was only a kid, what did I know?"

"Exactly," Sally said. "You didn't know enough to judge anyone. But you liked it here, had fun even, and were comfortable with the people who were living a lifestyle your mother ran away from. Cara's family. Others, too."

I couldn't keep the bitterness out of my voice. I put the mug down with a hard thunk. "So she stopped bringing me here because it made me happy?"

Sally shrugged. "I could be wrong. That was just my take.

You'd have to ask your mother if you want some real answers about what happened back then."

Sally went into the kitchen and I heard her opening cupboards and filling a kettle to make some tea. More than likely she was trying to give me some space to process what she'd just told me. It made sense—all of it. Charlie's inherent sadness was a result of a tragic accident, and the reason my mother ran from Bridgewater was because she didn't approve of the lifestyle.

But why would she deprive me of my friends and extended family? Then I remembered Sally's comment. *You'd have to ask your mother....*

Without thinking about what I'd say, I pulled my cell out of my back pocket. Shit. No service.

Going into the kitchen, I picked up the phone from the wall, dialed. It suddenly seemed urgent that I get some answers. "Hi, Mother," I said when she answered on the first ring.

"What's the crisis?"

"There's no crisis, I just—"

"Then why are you calling me in the middle of a work day? You never call during the week. Did something happen at work?"

"I'm not at work." I had to spit it out before she started in on her line of questioning. "I'm in Bridgewater."

The answering silence was brief but telling. It took a shock to shut my mother up for more than a heartbeat. "What are you doing in Bridgewater?"

I walked into the mud room by the back door, stretching the phone cord as far as it would go. "I have to deal with Charlie's house, remember?"

Another pause. "I figured you would have hired someone to clear it out and put it on the market. You didn't have to go there."

"I wanted to."

She sighed on the other end of the line. "You always did like that godforsaken place."

And now we were getting somewhere.

"Yeah, I did like it here. That's one of the reasons I'm calling, actually. I was curious about why we stopped coming."

The silence was too long this time. She really hadn't seen that one coming. "I take it you've been there long enough to see that Bridgewater is a unique place."

Unique was one word for it, but my mother managed to make that word sound like an insult. "It's definitely unique," I agreed.

She sighed again. "Okay, Catherine."

She was the first to call me Catherine in a few days. The name sounded weird now.

"What is it you really want to know? Did I grow up in an unorthodox family? Yes. Was Charlie in a polyamorous relationship? I imagine you've already learned the answer to that." Her voice was filled with impatience, which is pretty much how she sounded all the time, come to think of it.

"Why did we stop coming here?" I twirled the cord around my finger. "Stop seeing Uncle Charlie?"

"That is no lifestyle to expose an impressionable young girl to. You were getting old enough that you would have started to figure out what was going on, and your father and I didn't want that for you."

"God, Mom, you make it sound like the people of Bridgewater were performing satanic rituals or something."

Her tone hardened. "I know all about what goes on in that town, Catherine. I grew up there, remember? Had two fathers, even. I knew that what was going on around me, even in my own house, wasn't normal."

I toyed with a line of clothespins clipped to a string by the door and tried not to lose my temper. The anger welling up in my chest was tainted with sadness, regret. I'd been happy here, dammit. I'd been surrounded by people who cared about me more than they cared about their careers or their image. Yet, my mother had chosen to end that. "It may not be normal, but that doesn't automatically mean it's wrong."

"We didn't want that life for you. I still don't." Suspicion crept into her voice. "What is this about, Catherine?"

When I didn't answer right away, she continued. "Don't tell me you're thinking of staying there."

I opened my mouth to say *No, of course not. I have a job to get back to.* But the words wouldn't come.

"Catherine." She drew the word out as a warning, but I'd had enough. She'd confirmed what I'd suspected from the moment I'd learned about Bridgewater's unique ways. She'd kept me from this place for propriety's sake, even though it had made me happy. She was filling my head with her negative thoughts on the place even through the phone. Being here, meeting the people, seeing it with my own eyes, painted a different picture entirely.

"I've got to go, Mom. Good talking with you." It really wasn't, but I had no idea what else to say. I wasn't going to call her later. I wasn't even sure I really loved her. Not in a healthy, normal way.

I hung up before she could respond. I'd heard enough and walked the phone back to the wall base. Sally turned to me holding two mugs of tea, handed me one. "What did your mother say?"

I forced a rueful smile. "Nothing I hadn't already guessed." That she and my father had put image and propriety above everything else, including my happiness, Charlie's happiness, and a loving community. No wonder my mother had fled from this place—she'd always been looking for normalcy. Always cared more about fitting in than being loved. And that's what she'd wanted for me, too. A normal life. One that fit the ideal life she'd set her sights on. That she'd attained.

The sad thing was, in my mother's opinion, I was living the dream in New York. Sure, my marriage had been a bust, but what was one little divorce? Everybody who was anybody in the city had one of those under their belts. What mattered to her was how my life looked on paper, and on that count, I had it all. The Ivy League education, the law school diploma on the wall, an up-and-coming career at a leading firm... what did it matter that I was miserable? My day to day life was filled with work, stress, and more work, with the occasional trip to the gym to break up the monotony. Because one couldn't forget that the perfect body was also part of the deal. Looks mattered almost as much as income and job title. I'd bought into that hook, line and sinker. Until now.

God, the thought of going back to that was almost too depressing to bear.

My mother's words came back to me. *It wasn't normal.* She was right about that. Life in Bridgewater wasn't normal... but it was better. Better than the life I'd been leading in New York, at least. If I went back there, I'd be going back to day after day where I was too busy to meet a nice, single guy and go on a date, let alone have a meaningful relationship. Hell, my job in New York left me no time for a simple friendship outside of the office.

Less than a week in Bridgewater and I'd experienced more joy, friendship, laughter, and amazing sex than the last few years in New York. Maybe the people in this town had the right idea. They certainly had different priorities than most people I'd known in my life, but that didn't mean those priorities were wrong.

A smile tugged at the corner of my lips as I remembered Sam and Jack's means of helping me get my priorities straight. Especially the spanking. Sheesh, my ass was still a little sore. Other places, too. Maybe their particular techniques were working, after all. Because I sure as hell was starting to reconsider what was important to me. Not spanking, but the way they made me forget everything, to focus on what was really important. And it wasn't a corner office.

I'd be hard pressed to find a more caring group of people than those in Bridgewater. And Sam and Jack? My heart constricted in my chest at the thought of those two men. *My* men.

Yeah, they were definitely a priority.

But so was my career. I'd already invested a shitload of time and energy into getting where I was. Granted, I still wasn't partner, but I would be. All that hard work had to count for something, didn't it? I couldn't just throw all of that away. Could I?

Sally told me she had a potential buyer to meet at another property and with a quick wave she was out the door, leaving me alone with the clutter and my conflicted thoughts. Luckily intensive cleaning was a fantastic distraction, so I threw myself into it and didn't stop for the next hour.

I probably wouldn't have stopped then if it wasn't for Charlie's phone ringing. The man on the other end introduced himself as Buck Reinhardt. The name didn't ring a bell but from his arrogant tone and the expectant pause, I guessed it should have.

"What can I do for you, Buck?"

Turned out Buck Reinhardt was a pretty big deal in Montana real estate—or at least, he seemed to think so. He launched into a spiel about his company and all the development projects they had in the works. As he was talking, Sam and Jack knocked on the back door and walked in, making concentration difficult. Two sexy cowboys strutting around my kitchen and I had the attention span of a gnat.

As Buck yammered on in my ear, Jack sauntered over with that sexy grin of his and wrapped an arm around my waist, pulling me up against him so I could feel his hard cock pressing against his jeans. Sam leaned against the kitchen table beside me and gave me a wink.

"Do I have your attention, Catherine?" Buck asked in my ear.

"Um..." I gave Jack's chest a little shove but apparently, he took that as a request to start nibbling at my neck. I bit my lip to keep from moaning into the phone.

"I wasn't fortunate enough to know your uncle, but I've heard great things about him," Buck said.

"Mmhmm." Why was he still talking? And what was Jack doing with his tongue that made my knees give out like that?

"But I do think your uncle would have appreciated the New York City apartment you could purchase for the price I'm offering on his property."

My eyes sprang open. *Offer? What offer?*

Buck quoted a number then that made me gasp so loudly, Jack sprang back with surprise and Sam shot up straight. They hovered over me with questioning looks, but I waved them off as I asked Buck to repeat what he'd just said.

"The amount?"

"No, all of it. I was distracted."

Buck repeated himself and this time I listened, with Sam and Jack waiting impatiently nearby. By the time I hung up, they were pacing the kitchen. "What was that about?" Sam asked. "Was it your ex? Chad? Because he and I had a little chat and he won't be bothering you any more."

I frowned at him wondering what he'd done, what he'd said to Chad, but I was distracted by Buck's offer to think on it further.

"No, not Chad. A real estate developer."

I told them what he'd told me—how he wanted to buy Charlie's property, along with his water rights, for a sum that made my stomach do backflips. Holy shit, I could buy myself a partnership with that kind of money. Hell, I could buy the firm.

Well, maybe that was an exaggeration, but it was a hell of a lot of money—more than I'd be able to save in a decade at my current salary. Buck had been right, I could buy property in the city. No more shoebox apartment. For an investor, he'd done his research and worked his sales pitch to where it would be most enticing.

Jack muttered a "hot damn" at the sum and Sam slid down into a kitchen chair. By his grim expression, I had a feeling he'd gone into lawyer mode, thinking through every angle of this deal.

I knew, because I'd done the same thing. As soon as my stomach settled down, my brain raced into action trying to sort through possible pitfalls, the legal ramifications, what to do next, and what this deal would mean for me.

"Are you going to take the offer?" Jack asked. My gaze met Sam's.

He knew what I was going to say and he beat me to it. "She needs to do her homework at city hall first. Isn't that right, doll?"

I was already gathering up my purse and car keys as I nodded. To Jack, I explained, "I can't even start to consider the deal until I sort out the details of this property's water rights and what they're worth. It's Old West laws I know nothing about."

He scratched his chin as he stared at the ground. I could tell he wanted to ask more questions and I had a good idea where they would lead. *What then?* If I sold, or even if I didn't... what then? Would I stay or would I go?

I didn't want to hear the questions because I didn't have the answers. I was even more confused than before. Instead of sticking around, I busted my ass trying to get out of there, ignoring the tension in the room.

"Do you want me to come with you?" Sam asked. "I could give you a ride, help you do some research."

I gave him an appreciative smile, but shook my head. "Thanks, but I need to do this on my own. Could you guys lock up when you leave?"

I'd almost reached the door when Jack's voice stopped me. "Sam and I will stick around and clear out some of this mess," he said, gesturing toward a stack of boxes and filled trash bags. "When you're done doing whatever it is you need to do, we'll meet you at Sam's house, got it?"

I nodded. It wasn't a request, really, but a command. I'd gotten used to Sam being the one who issued commands but Jack was a natural. He sauntered across the room until he was standing right in front of me, and placed a finger under my chin to tip my head up so I couldn't avoid his gaze.

"Don't make us wait, sweetness. There's a lot we need to discuss."

Shit. I knew exactly what they wanted to talk about, but I wasn't ready. "I thought you said you wouldn't pressure me."

He flashed me that shit-eating grin of his as he tugged me toward him roughly. "Did I say that?"

Oh fuck. He slipped a hand down the waistband of my jeans and cupped my pussy, using his fingers to tease my clit through the thin fabric of my panties. My whimper made him smile again and I heard Sam get out of his chair to join us.

"We won't pressure you, doll," Sam said, coming to stand behind me so I was sandwiched between them. Trapped in the best way possible. There was no place I'd rather be.

"Not everything can be solved by good sex," I countered, trying to keep my focus which was close to impossible with these two.

"Just *good*?" Jack countered.

Sam wrapped his arms around me, his hands cupping my breasts through my T-shirt. My nipples pressed against the fabric of my bra as his thumbs teased them and I found myself pushing against his palms, trying to get him to touch me harder, the way I liked.

He wouldn't, and I knew that was on purpose. These men loved to tease, to build up anticipation. I bit back a moan.

What they were doing was working.

"We won't push you," Sam said. His hands fell away, but Jack made no move to release me. His palm was still firmly pressed against my pussy and if he didn't stop working his fingers, I'd come for him just like that—standing and fully clothed. "And we won't use sex like a weapon. But you have to keep in mind how much we want you. Mind and body. This conversation? You can't put it off indefinitely."

No, I couldn't. Time was running out on this trip, which meant the clock was ticking on our relationship. "Not indefinitely," I agreed, my voice coming out irritatingly breathy. How was a person supposed to argue effectively when she was being manhandled from all directions?

As much as I wanted to give in and let them have their way with me in the kitchen, time wouldn't allow it. "But not now," I said. "I need to get to city hall before they close for the day."

"Not so fast, sweetness." Jack leaned down so I could feel his breath against my neck. "You're not going anywhere with those panties on."

14

ATHERINE

A little while later, I was going commando as I walked into
Bridgewater's town hall. I was also a good deal more relaxed than
I'd been that morning since they'd made sure to give me two
orgasms before sending me on my way. Jack hadn't stopped
fingering my pussy until I came right there in the doorway. After
that they'd ordered me to strip off my jeans so I could lose the
panties. Sam, apparently not content to let his cousin give me an
orgasm without giving me one as well, dropped to his knees and
buried his face between my thighs and started flicking my clit with
his tongue, making me come fast and furious as I leaned against
the kitchen counter.

So much for not using sex as a weapon. A very pleasurable,
mind blowing weapon.

I was sure everyone I passed in city hall could see that I was
glowing, but I didn't have time to worry about gossip. The building
was only open for another hour and I needed the legal

information so I could make an informed decision. Buck hadn't pressured me to give him an answer immediately, but I wanted to figure out what I was doing with Charlie's property as soon as possible. It was too much of a mess to get it ready for market in the next few days, so I'd have no time to think about it if I went back to New York.

If I went back. Since when had I started to doubt my return? For a little while now, if I was being honest. Hell, I'd started to have my doubts about heading back to New York after that first night with Sam and Jack. And who wouldn't? There was never any question that being wanted by two sexy cowboys was a temptation. I wouldn't have been a badge carrying woman if I didn't at least think about staying.

But being tempted didn't mean it was the right choice. I still had responsibilities and a life to get back to.

The clerk in the records department helped me find all the information I needed in about five minutes. I took the next half hour to read through it all at a small counter and then read it all again. After I was done, I called Sally and asked her some questions to make sure I'd understood the details. Real estate law was fascinating, especially since I had such a personal case.

As I hung up from Sally, I knew any hope of being an overnight millionaire vanished before my eyes. No fancy apartment in New York. Turned out Charlie's water rights were not only senior, but affected most of the ranches in the county. What was done to Charlie's land had long term, lasting impacts. Basically, by taking Buck's offer, I'd be screwing over all the properties downstream of Charlie—and that was most of the land west of Bridgewater.

I left city hall just before closing and headed straight toward Sam's place downtown. I'd been warned about being late, but that wasn't why I rushed. I had my answers. While I didn't know what to do with the land, it didn't matter. Not right this second. Truth was, I couldn't wait to see them again. God, I couldn't be away from them for an hour without missing them.

About halfway to his place, my cell rang and I answered it on speaker without looking to see who it was. The streets were straight and I only passed a few cars, but I still didn't want to take my eyes from the road. I should have looked. I really should have checked.

"Just called to say thank you, Catherine."

Roberts. Crap.

A call from the case stealing lawyer was exactly what my day did not need. But it was his nasally New York accent that filled my car and had my hands clenching the steering wheel in annoyance. "What do you want, Roberts?"

"No need to bite my head off."

There was no way I'd give him the satisfaction of asking what he was talking about. His smug tone said enough. I didn't cut him off quickly enough, because he continued uninterrupted. "I guess you heard that I settled the Marsden case. Farber was pleased with the outcome, as I'm sure he told you."

Fuck. I slammed a fist against the steering wheel. "That's *my* case."

"*Was* your case." There was no denying the laughter in his voice. "Thanks again for taking a vacation. Please, feel free to stay as long as you'd like. Where are you? Bumfuck, Montana? I hear cow tipping's tons of fun. I've got your cases handled, so just—"

I hung up on the prick before he could finish. My fingers gripped the steering wheel so hard my knuckles turned white, my blood pressure probably on its way to stroke level. I had to get back. *Now*. The sooner the better. I couldn't waste any more time in the middle of nowhere while my cases were being stolen out from under me. Panic made my heart race. Every minute I was here was another chance for Roberts to take credit for my work. If I didn't get back now, I'd lose out on the partnership for good.

Breathe in. Breathe out. Goddammit, breathing exercises were a useless waste of time when I was seething with anger. No amount of controlled breaths would give me the release I needed.

But Sam and Jack could. They knew how to make me forget, make me let go of all the shit in my life and just... be. Just come again and again. Yes, I needed to fuck. I needed orgasms. Thank god I was headed to them now or I might combust. And when I was back in New York? What would I do then? Book a flight to Montana every time the stress got to be too much? It was a long way for a booty call.

I could quit. The thought resonated like a gong. I could say goodbye to the stress and the competition and live life like the people of Bridgewater—surrounded by friends, enjoying life. Being loved.

I could be a lawyer in Montana. Sam did it. Why couldn't I? But *would* I? It would mean giving up everything I'd been working toward, everything I'd thought I'd wanted for so long. Was I ready to make that sacrifice for the Kanes?

As I pulled into Sam's driveway, I still didn't have an answer.

————

SAM

Jack and I hauled a truckload of boxes out of Charlie's house and took them to the dump before coming back to my place to wait on Katie. Manual labor had been a great distraction from the elephant in the room but now we had nothing to do but sit and wait.

"You don't look nervous," I said. Not that Jack typically looked nervous; he was easygoing by nature. But this was hardly a normal situation. It wasn't every day we asked a woman to be ours. We hadn't used the word *wife*, not yet at least, but it was implied. It was what we meant and what we wanted. Katie as our wife, mother of our children.

I couldn't remember the last time I wanted something more. This was nothing like Samantha Connors, my high school sweetheart. I could see now that Jack had been right to turn away from that. She hadn't been the one for us.

Katie was.

"That's because I'm *not* nervous," Jack said. He sank into the couch and sprawled out, stretched his long legs out in front of him. "Katie loves it here in Bridgewater. She'll stay."

I kicked his boots off the couch so I could sit too. "I wish I had your confidence."

He arched an eyebrow at me. "You don't think she loves it here?"

"I know she does. But deciding to stay means getting out of her own head for more than two seconds and listening to her gut."

Jack gave a little grunt of agreement. He knew I was right. Did Katie love Bridgewater? Hell, yes. Did she enjoy spending time with us? Absolutely. That woman couldn't doubt that she was our perfect match in bed—and out—at least. We'd made our point there... we'd showed her just how good it could be. But just because she enjoyed hot sex didn't mean she was ready to admit that she belonged with us. It sure as hell didn't mean she was ready to commit to being with us for the rest of her life.

Jack seemed to read my mind. He shifted so he could lean forward, his gaze unusually intense. "Look, Sam, we don't need her to agree to marry us—not today, at least. We just need her to stay. If she does that...."

He had a point. If she stayed, we would win her in the end. If she wanted courting, we'd do it. Roses, candlelight, horseback rides. Whatever. This had been fast and that damn lightning wasn't something she believed in. That was okay. If she stayed, we'd have all the time in the world to have her fall in love with us.

"You're right," I said.

He grinned. "Of course, I am."

I kept thinking of the way her eyes had lit up during dinner at Cara's the other night. She'd been luminous and in her element. Laughing and talking, she'd been relaxed and content—a far cry from the tightly wound ball of stress I'd met that first day at the bar. She deserved to be like that all the time, not just when she was on vacation.

That right there was what I was afraid of. She saw all of this as a vacation from life. A hot fling, a leisurely pace, fun with friends —I had a horrible feeling that in her mind this was all just a break from "real" life. Perhaps even a distraction, something keeping her from the fast lane, the corner office. Maybe I was wrong and Jack was right. Maybe she was coming around to the idea of staying. There had definitely been moments when I'd thought she had, but then there were times when I could see her mind drifting back to New York and all the bullshit that waited for her there. It was hard to fight against a cell phone, instant messaging, emails and a type-A personality.

Much as I might want to trust that Jack was right, I knew better. Our Katie was torn in two and there was no telling which way she'd go in the end.

I didn't feel any better about the situation when she arrived looking frazzled and irritated. Gone was the sweetly satisfied woman who'd let me eat her pussy in her kitchen a few hours ago. What the hell had happened in that time to make her look so rattled?

Jack gave a quick questioning look as she strode past him into the living area and I shrugged in response. Something was up, that much was obvious. Whether that something worked in our favor or not was impossible to tell.

"What's going on, doll?" I came up behind her and took her purse from her shoulder, setting it on an end table so I could rub her shoulders and neck. Sure enough, she was a bundle of knots. Before she opened her mouth, I had a good idea what she was going to say. There was one name I was starting to hate because it was bound to have this effect on her.

"Fucking Roberts," she spit out.

Jack groaned and fell back onto the couch. I couldn't blame him, at this point it felt like we were beating our heads against a brick wall trying to get Katie to face the fact that her life back in New York was toxic and unfulfilling. At least I'd tracked down her ex and called him. Chatted about his behavior. Chatted, and when he wasn't as accommodating as I'd wanted, threatened a stalking charge, a restraining order, both of which would be public record and something the senior partners at Barker, Paul and Cambridge might be interested in. After that, we'd seen eye-to-eye and I was satisfied he could be crossed off Katie's list of jackasses. But Roberts? The only way he was going to go away was if Katie did. To Bridgewater, permanently.

"What did he do now?" Jack asked.

I inwardly groaned, wishing he hadn't. I hated seeing Katie so worked up over that asshole thousands of miles away. If he could fuck with her at such a distance, I had to wonder what he was like in person.

Before she could launch into a tirade about whatever the fucker had done this time, I cut in. "What did you find out at city hall?"

She blinked in surprise and I could practically see the gears shifting in her head. This was why she and I worked. We thought alike, were able to multitask to the extreme. I knew how to push her buttons—challenge her, make her think. And she did the same for me. I looked over to see Jack take a swig of his beer as he lounged on the couch.

Thank God we had Jack to round us out. To make us remember that life was sometimes pretty damn simple. The perfect threesome. Well, pretty damn close to perfect anyway.

Katie reached for Jack's beer, taking it out of his hand and making him laugh as she drained the rest of it. Then she turned to me. "It was eye opening, I can tell you that."

She recounted what she'd learned and at the end, Jack let out a low whistle. Being a rancher, he knew water rights inside and out. I knew them from a legal perspective, knew what Katie now owned—controlled—without having to go to city hall. "Wow, that's some power you've got there."

"You could make half the ranches in the county go belly up." Just over something as simple and basic as water. I should have kept my mouth shut, judging from the glare I got from her.

"What are you going to do?" Jack watched Katie with a look I knew well. It was the same look he gave me every time he was giving me shit... playing devil's advocate. He knew damned well Katie wouldn't do anything to hurt this town or the people in it— because she loved it here. But he wanted her to admit that simple fact. Maybe then she would admit that she wanted to stay, that she belonged in Bridgewater.

Shit, sometimes my cousin was smarter than he looked.

Right on cue, Katie got all riled, worse than when she'd first arrived. "What do you mean, what am I going to do?"

"It's a lot of money, doll." I took a step toward her, putting my life on the line judging by that glare. "No one would blame you if you were tempted to take the deal."

Her jaw fell open and she stalked over to me, closing the distance between us. Stabbing a finger into my chest, she said, "How can you even say that? Do you know what would happen if I sold to that developer?"

"You'd be stinking rich?"

She stiffened up like a rod and Jack grinned.

She whirled around so quickly her hair whipped my face. "And I'd screw everyone in this town over in the process." Shaking her head, she backed up so she could face us both, her arms crossed in front of her chest.

"Now simmer down, doll."

Those words had the exact opposite effect I wanted. I wouldn't have been surprised to see smoke coming out her ears at that point. Surely, she had to see it now. It had to be obvious that she cared about this town and its people. She couldn't walk away from it any more than me or Jack could. This town was in our blood and where we belonged, and it was the same for Katie.

She belonged with us, here in Bridgewater. Now she just had to say it.

"And if I don't, are you going to spank me?"

Those were fighting words.

"Hell, no. Spanking's for when you need a good fucking and your mind's elsewhere. This?" I waved a hand at her. "This is you using that smart brain of yours."

"Then don't tell me to simmer down. I have every right to be mad at you two. If you two think I could do that—hurt all those people and destroy Charlie's legacy in the process..." She shook her head and grabbed her purse. "If you think that, then clearly you don't know me as well as I thought."

She bolted for the door before we could stop her.

"Clearly, you don't know me at all."

15

ATHERINE

Tears were blinding me, making it hard to see the road as I drove back to Charlie's to grab my things. My cell was ringing, but for once, I ignored it. If it was Roberts, I'd probably go postal. But he'd done his damage for the day. It was Sam and Jack. I knew it, but I didn't want to talk to them. Not now.

I swiped at the tears as I ran inside and threw my belongings into my suitcase. I hated crying, always had. I'd overreacted back there and I knew it. But still, the fact that Sam and Jack thought so little of me hurt more than I cared to admit. I might not want to stay in Bridgewater, but that didn't mean I wanted to hurt the people who'd only been nice to me. Yeah, I was a ruthless lawyer, but I wasn't heartless.

I'd known then and there that it was time for me to go. Those two had been my weakness—to think I'd almost considered staying for them had me jamming my makeup into the toiletry case with more force than needed. When I walked into Sam's house, a little part of me had actually been hoping they'd convince me to stay. Okay, a big part.

I just wanted someone—no, two someones—to want me for me.

Anger had my hands shaking as I wadded up clothes and threw them into the luggage. First Roberts rubbed my face in the fact that he'd stolen my case and then Sam and Jack basically accused me of being a money-hungry, callous bitch.

That made up my mind for me and I sped down the two-lane highway toward the Bozeman airport. I wouldn't stay here if that's the way they felt and I glanced in my rearview mirror as the lights of Bridgewater faded away. Lightning strike, my ass. Besides, I had to get back now or risk losing my chance at the partnership once and for all. I could get a flight to Denver tonight, then be on the first flight to New York in the morning. Maybe there'd even be a red eye. I'd be in the office by nine. This was the right decision. The inevitable choice. I'd always put career first and nothing had changed that, especially since two hot cowboys weren't standing in the way any longer.

I was far too early for my flight so I went to the airport's one restaurant with the view of the runway and the mountains in the distance. At the bar, I ordered a wine and settled in to wait. I downed the first glass trying to quell the churning pit in my stomach. My mind kept flip flopping between the job I was heading back to and the could-be life I was leaving behind in Montana. I ricocheted back and forth between stress and an aching loneliness.

Shit, where the hell was the bartender with my second glass?

Elaine called while I was waiting. Seriously, how long did it take to open a new bottle? Her familiar voice should have been a comfort, but at that particular moment, it was another reminder of what I was going back to. The catty office backstabbing, the alliances and the battles as if we were in some sort of battle to the death and not co-workers at the same firm. Roberts was ruthless, vindictive and had zero ethics. Perfect for a lawyer.

"Did you hear the news?" she asked as soon as I answered.

"I'm fine, thanks for asking. And how are you?" The bartender came over, filled my glass all the way to the top. When I glanced up, he tilted his head toward my phone, then winked.

She ignored my lame attempt at a joke. "Roberts is telling anyone who will listen that you're too soft to be partner. Can you believe that jackass? He told Ronald that he'd scared you off and—"

"I've got to go, Elaine. My flight is boarding." I clicked 'end call' before she could respond and took a gulp of my wine. I still had an hour before I had to get to my gate but I couldn't listen anymore. I just couldn't. And not because I was so angry but because I just didn't care anymore. I'd hit my limit on caring about this shit. It all suddenly seemed ridiculous. Juvenile, even. New York seemed a million miles away and that's where I wanted to keep it.

I. Didn't. Care.

Freedom washed over me in an exhilarating rush. Fuck that place. Fuck Roberts. Fuck Farber. They could all suck a dick.

It was like I'd just torn off a pair of blinders and could see clearly for the first time in forever. Why was I going back there? For what? A job that wasn't rewarding in the slightest, a firm that didn't value me in any real way, a life without friends besides Elaine or lovers who knew exactly what buttons to push to make me hot, to make me scream. A love life without one boyfriend, let alone two. Why would I choose that over what I had here?

In Bridgewater, I had a family legacy. I had roots. I had a town full of people who seemed to truly care about me. Maybe most importantly, I had something a lot like love.

Holy shit. *Love.*

The thought of Sam and Jack made my heart squeeze in my chest. Maybe they were right and what we had was the real deal.

I'd felt more in just a few days than I had my entire marriage with Chad. The only way I would know for sure was if I saw this through, whatever the hell it was. I remembered Jack's term, lightning. Could lightning strike at an airport bar?

The bartender grinned broadly as he held up the wine bottle, silently asking if I wanted more. I belatedly realized he was returning my smile that wasn't brought on by the wine. I was beaming like a goddamn moron and I didn't care.

Yes, I was soft just as Roberts was telling everyone. I wasn't ruthless. I was nice. Thoughtful. Caring. And I had two men who liked me that way.

That was it. I was done with New York. I was done with misogynist assholes like Roberts and Farber. It was time to say goodbye to a lonely, loveless meaningless existence of competition and struggle. Of a shoebox apartment and trade it in for big skies and bigger men.

Instead of signaling for a refill, I asked for the check.

Adrenaline gave me more of a buzz than the wine. I was really doing this; I was going to quit my job. Better yet, I was going to stay in Bridgewater.

I picked up my cell again before I could overthink it. Just as Jack and Sam had been trying to get me to do, I just stopped analyzing and worrying. I was tired of my fear and insecurities changing my mind and I didn't want to do that. I had to be brave and follow my gut and my heart for once in my life, otherwise I'd end up miserable and loveless like my mother.

My fingers shook as I searched for Sally's contact info and called her. "Sally? Sorry to call after hours. Listen, there's been a change of plans. I'm not ready to sell. Not yet, at least." Her whoop of joy had me holding the phone away from my ear. Seemed she and Violet Kane had been waiting for this call ever since they met me.

After hanging up with Sally I hurried to the gate to have them get my checked bag back. It took talking to two counter representatives, a flight attendant and a manager but I eventually got my bag and told them I'd eat the cost of my ticket.

Fuck my flight, I was going home.

To Bridgewater. To the rooster clock and the hobo figurines.

I din't think I'd ever felt lighter than I did walking away from that counter, wheeling my bag behind me. I didn't let myself worry about what I was going to say to Farber when I called him in the morning, or what my parents would think about my decision. All I cared about was getting back to Sam and Jack.

I had to apologize. God, I was such an idiot. I'd been so pissed that they'd thought I'd prioritize money and prestige over Bridgewater and its residents. But why wouldn't they think that? I hadn't known them long and in that time I'd repeatedly chosen work over everything else. They'd spanked me enough times for it. That stopped now. Not the spankings, those were actually pretty hot.

They'd spent so much time showing me what my priorities should be, and I'd been too stubborn to see it. Well, not anymore. I picked up my pace as I headed toward the sliding doors. Now, it was my turn to show them what really mattered to me. I'd nearly reached the exit when I came to a stop. There were my men walking in, looking ridiculously hot. My heart leapt into my throat at the sight of them.

My men. I loved the sound of that. It felt right, just like it felt right when they told me I was their woman. We fit together—now I just had to show them that I'd finally learned my lesson.

16

$\mathcal{J}$ACK

I heard Sam's sigh of relief as we walked through the airport entrance and spotted Katie. Thank god we caught her before she flew back to New York. We'd wasted too much time debating what we should do after she ran out on us. Sam and I had gotten into an argument over who was to blame for her taking off like that. He'd thought we'd pushed her too hard, but I'd been certain that pushing her was the only way we could get her to open her eyes and see what was right in front of her face.

It wasn't that simple. It had taken Sam his dad's heart attack to come home and realize what he truly wanted. Katie had to put value to her rat race life and decide if it was worth it. For some, the decision wasn't fast and Katie was so damn smart she'd analyze every bit of it before she worked it out. Having the two of us loom and push her, spank her ass, wasn't going to help.

We'd just agreed that we would give her space for the rest of

144

the night when Cara called and told us that Katie had sent her a text with instructions on where to find Charlie's house key. It seemed our Katie had taken off. Bolted. She'd made her decision.

There went the idea of giving her space. Sam and I didn't waste time talking it over, we ran out, hopped into my truck and sped to the airport. On the way, we'd both realized the one thing we hadn't told her was that we were in love with her. We weren't just two cowboys looking to scratch her itch. We weren't two men who wanted a woman. No, we wanted her because our hearts belonged to her. Perhaps if we'd led with that, maybe we wouldn't have needed to chase after her.

The moment we entered the terminal, we saw her.

I turned to Sam with a grin. It looked like we'd made it just in time.

She was rushing toward us, pulling her suitcase behind her, but she stopped short at the sight of us. For a second there, I thought about throwing her over my shoulder and taking her home. She was meant to be with us and if she didn't realize that by now, she sure as hell would after we fucked her brains out all night. But we'd been doing the caveman routine ever since we met her. Yes, she needed dominant men in her life since while she was smart and headstrong and a damn fine lawyer, she was also submissive. We'd been trying to clear her mind of her insanity, but we'd also kept her from working through it all. It took every ounce of my control to let her have the space she needed to figure it out, just as long as she didn't get on that damn plane.

The blank look of surprise on her face was replaced by a giant smile and all the tension eased out of my body at that gorgeous sight. Sam came up beside me and muttered, "Thank God."

Amen to that. A second later and she ditched the bag and came running over to us. I caught her in my arms and swooped her up so I could plant a kiss on those soft lips. I crushed her to me, hoping she could feel everything I couldn't say just then. Like how terrified I'd been that she'd left for good, and how glad I was that she'd come to her senses.

She kissed me back with that fiery intensity of hers before wiggling her body so she could slither down to the ground. Sam caught her the moment her feet touched the terminal floor and pulled her into an embrace of his own.

Sam never was one to be outdone. Especially not by me.

After they shared a kiss that nearly set off the sprinklers, I tapped him on the shoulder and he pulled back, letting a dazed Katie stumble back into my arms. I wrapped an arm around her waist to hold her upright. "Going somewhere, sweetness?"

Fuck, I hoped not.

She shook her head. "Not anymore."

Sam stepped forward to reach a hand out and brush her cheek. "Were you crying, doll?"

Nodding, she said, "I was upset. It was stupid."

I exchanged a look with Sam. I'd learned my lesson on pushing Katie too hard, but he gave me a nod. "So, since you're not on your flight, does that mean you're going to stay here a little longer?"

"No."

What the hell? For the first time, it occurred to me that maybe her flight was just delayed. Or maybe she'd booked a later flight.

Her smile was slow and sweet. "I'm staying for good."

Sam let out a whoop that had a guy in jeans and a camo t-shirt staring and I lifted Katie up for another kiss. When I set her back down, she looked up at us in confusion. "What are you guys doing here?"

"We came to get you," Sam said. "Cara told us you took off."

"If we were too late, we were ready to buy tickets to New York," I added. I took her hand in mine. "I'm sorry, Katie. Back at the house, we were tough on you. Maybe too tough."

She shook her head quickly. "No, you weren't."

Sam wouldn't let her finish. "We were. But it was only because we wanted you to see that you love it here."

"We knew you would never sell to that developer," I said.

Tears welled up in her eyes and it was all I could do not to pick her up again and this time never let her go.

"Really? You knew that I would make the right decision?"

Sam scoffed. "Of course. We may not have known you for long, but we do know you."

"There was no doubt in my mind," I said. "We just needed you to realize how much you care about Bridgewater."

She nodded. "I do care about Bridgewater." Dropping her head, she peeked up at us from beneath lowered lashes. "And you. *Both* of you."

Sam wrapped an arm around her shoulders and I squeezed her waist. At that moment, it all seemed to click into place—for me, at least. With Katie nestled against my side, and Sam beside her, this was where we were meant to be. *This.* We were a team, just the way our relatives before us had intended.

We were also making a scene. The airport wasn't crowded but we'd been carrying on as if we were alone in a bubble and not smack dab in the middle of a public place.

"Maybe we should take this elsewhere," Sam said. He went to grab the abandoned luggage while I entwined my hand with Katie's and led her toward the exit.

Sam caught up to us as we were crossing the parking lot toward my truck.

"I returned my rental car," Katie said, as if there was any doubt that she'd be coming home with us.

"We'll have to look into getting you a car," Sam said. "You can't use a rental forever."

Forever. The word hung out there in the fresh summer air. For a second I felt sure she would bolt again. I knew that skittish colt look when I saw it. Taking a deep breath, she added, "Yeah, I guess you're right. Where does a girl go to find a used car around here?"

Just like that, the spooked look was gone. Maybe she wanted this new life after all.

We reached the truck when Katie stopped and looked up at us. "I know what I've been saying all along… about how much I needed that promotion and how important it was that I go back."

I exchanged a quick look with Sam. Where was this going?

"I get it if you don't trust me or this decision." Her expression was so serious, it looked like she was about to break some terrible news. "But I know what I'm doing. I may have had my priorities all messed up before, but they're clear now. I'm staying in Bridgewater, it's where I belong."

I grinned at Sam before turning back to her. "We know that, sweetness."

Sam cut in. "You don't have to apologize for not seeing it right away. You weren't raised here and this is all new to you. We don't expect you to adapt overnight."

I skimmed my palm down her back and squeezed that plump ass of hers playfully. "You've got plenty of nights to get used to this idea."

I wanted to tell her how I felt, to let Sam take the time to do the same, but the airport parking lot wasn't the place to do it.

She laughed as I handed her up into the truck. When she turned to smile down at me, the rightness of it had me grinning back at her. I'd known she was the one ever since that plane ride. When she'd accidentally straddled me, everything in me had said *she's the one*. I knew Sam had the same experience the moment he'd spotted her at the bar. But we'd been raised in Bridgewater so finding the one and knowing it instantly… that wasn't a foreign concept for us. But Katie? She'd had to learn to trust her heart. And us.

I climbed up to sit beside her, my cock growing hard just

thinking of all the ways we would reward her for making the right decision, to show her how we felt.

Sam took his seat on the other side of Katie after loading her luggage in the back. I saw his hand reach out and caress her bare thigh just above her knee where her skirt stopped. Yup, my cousin and I were on the same page, all right.

I'd learned my lesson about pressuring this woman, though, and wouldn't do it again. I stroked her leg where it pressed against mine and gave it a little squeeze. "Listen, sweetness. *We* know that you're the one for us and we're pretty headstrong about it. You can take your time coming around to that realization, just as long as you don't run off. We won't push you again."

Sam nodded. "We tried to throw you head first into the deep end with all this talk of being *the one*, didn't we? From here on out, we promise to let you ease into the idea."

Katie was quiet for a few moments, her eyes fixed on the sight of our hands on her thighs. She reached down and grabbed a hold of our hands and squeezed. "Thank you. Really. I appreciate that." She turned to glance up at me and then Sam, then slid her hands up the tops of her thighs, her skirt riding up with it. I'd pulled out of the parking spot, but was still in the lot. I slammed on the brakes to watch what she was doing. I moved my hand from her leg, so did Sam. Lifting her hips, she shimmied out of her lavender and lace panties, worked them down her legs. Holding them up in the air, the delicate fabric dangled from her finger as she spread her knees wider and exposing her pussy. "But if you don't mind, I'd rather you ease me right into bed."

Sam growled and snatched her panties, put his hand on her knee. "Good girl, Katie."

Putting my hand on her other knee, we kept her pussy exposed as I pressed my foot to the accelerator and sped toward my ranch like the devil was on our tail.

17

ATHERINE

By the time we got to Jack's ranch, I was on fire. It could have been the rush of adrenaline and the heady elation at seeing Sam and Jack at the airport that had me be so bold, but no. It was that they'd been right all along. Yes, they were demanding and bossy as hell, but I needed it. *Wanted* it. I wanted them. So when I tugged off my panties and held them out for them, it was a sign, albeit a very naughty one, that I was giving myself to them. To let them know I was submitting to them. I wanted to be between them, the rest of the world slipping away. No, going commando wasn't going to make my problems go away, but it was a reminder that I had Jack and Sam. I wasn't alone any more.

When Jack turned off his truck in front of his house, I was vibrating with pent up emotions. Luckily, I had my men to help me with that.

My men. I was starting to get used to the idea, slowly but surely. I'd tell them that. But for now, all I wanted was to show them.

"Jack," I said as we walked into his house, his arm about my waist. "When exactly was it that you knew I was the one?"

His slow smile said he knew exactly where I was going with this. Falling back onto the couch, he patted his lap. "I believe you were right about here."

Sam leaned against the doorframe as he watched me as I undid the zipper on my skirt, slid it down my feet to let it fall to the floor, bare from the waist down. I straddled Jack. "Here?" I asked.

"Mmm hmm." His hands came up to grip my thighs and from where I stood I could see the thick bulge of his cock pressing against his jeans. "On that plane, all I could think about was how I wanted to shove aside your panties and pull you down to sit on my cock. But bare is better."

I bit back a groan—who would have thought we'd had the same fantasy? I couldn't wait any longer. "Do you know what I wanted to do?"

"Show me." His eyelids were heavy with desire as he watched me unbutton his jeans and pull down his zipper. He lifted his hips so I could pull his jeans down low enough to pull out that long, thick cock. He grabbed a condom from his pocket and slid it on with deft fingers.

Leaning down, I whispered in his ear. "I wanted to ride you, cowboy."

"Now's your chance, sweetness. Climb on and ride me dirty. Yeah, just like that."

Settling one knee on either side of his hips, I hovered over his hard cock, then lowered myself to take him into my pussy in one quick movement. I was so wet from being open to them in the truck, the feel of him so thick and deep had me gasping for air. Jack's growl was low and primitive and before I knew what was happening his hands came to my hips and gripped me hard. He took over, rocking to pump that cock into me hard and fast.

I'd never seen Jack lose control... but I liked it. I turned my head to make sure Sam was watching. Sure enough, his dark gaze was on me and my pussy grew wetter than ever knowing he was turned on by the sight of me riding his cousin. I flicked my gaze down to his erection and licked my lips.

He didn't need any more of a hint. "Did your fantasy include two men at the same time?"

Slowly, I shook my head and crooked my finger. "Who wants a fantasy when I can have the real thing?"

As Jack fucked me, Sam came over, stripped off my blouse and bra so I was completely bare.

Clenching down, I tortured Jack's cock as Sam found a condom and lube, sheathed himself and then liberally coated it with lube. With slick fingers, he touched my back entrance as Jack stilled. While gentle, his touch was cold and slick and I gasped.

"Shit, hurry, Sam. I need to move." Jack's voice was nothing more than a growl.

Sam worked his finger carefully into me, coating me and preparing me for his cock. He would be bigger than any of the plugs we'd played with, but I knew it would be so much better.

Jack's hands tightened on my hips and he lifted and lowered me, working me on his cock as Sam added more and more lube.

"Feel good?" Jack asked. The corner of his mouth tipped up, but I could tell he was on the brink. Neither man was one to hold back.

I nodded, licked my lips.

Sam's finger slipped free and I felt empty, even with Jack so deep. But it wasn't for long because Sam's cock was nudging me, pressing in. A warm hand settled on my shoulder.

"Breathe, doll. That's it, good girl."

It was hard to relax, but I knew it was the only way this was going to work. I lifted my gaze to Jack's, held it as Sam pressed forward. More and more until all at once that broad head popped inside. I gasped at the stretch, at the feel of him. Of *both* of them.

"Holy shit," I whispered, trying to wiggle my hips. It was... wow. Big. Intense.

I could hear Sam's ragged breathing as he slowly slid in and out, going deeper each time. Jack's hands slid up my body to cup my breasts, gently pluck the nipples.

"It's too much," I breathed.

"Shh," Jack crooned. "Close your eyes. Feel."

"I'm in. Fuck, doll, you're perfect," Sam said.

"Yes," I breathed. "This? Us? It's... God, I never knew it could be like this."

"Ready?" Jack asked.

I nodded, but I knew he was talking to Sam.

"Time to make you ours, doll."

Sam pulled back and Jack lifted his hips, filling me. Then they alternated, Jack pulling out and Sam sliding in all the way. They kept doing that and I slumped forward onto Jack's chest. I was the filling in a Kane boys sandwich and it was... incredible. Pinned between them, all I could do was surrender myself to the ride and trust that they would take care of me.

"Okay, sweetness?" Jack asked.

"Mmm," I murmured.

My eyes were closed and I did as Jack said, just felt. How could I not? I was so open, so filled, so... taken. Sweat coated my skin, the dark scent of fucking filled the air. It was too much. The feelings were explosive and I came, crying out and clenching down on both of them.

Jack thrust up one last time, shouting his release. Sam gripped my shoulder, slid out and then plunged deep. He, too, came.

I couldn't move if I tried. Not because I was skewered on two cocks, but because the orgasm had been that good. I wasn't sure if I had any bones left.

Later, when we were all sprawled on the couch recuperating—naked, because who needed clothes?—they asked if I'd eaten. "No, but I'm not hungry. I *am* dirty, though."

"No one ever doubted that," Sam said as he gave my ass a little slap.

"Not that kind of dirty," I laughed. "I never showered after all that cleaning this morning. And now this...." I waved a hand toward my body. I'd been used and used well. I was sticky and sweaty and lube still lingered in places that were a little sore. I was still desperately in need of a shower.

Luckily for me, Jack had a shower big enough for three. I was physically exhausted after a long day of cleaning, packing, and fucking. Not to mention the emotional exhaustion from the roller coaster of my emotions. Sam and Jack handled me like a priceless doll, helping me into the shower. I just stood there and let them pamper me—Sam in front and Jack in back as they lathered up some soap and scrubbed me down, massaging my aching muscles as they went. How had I ever thought I could walk away from this?

When I was nice and clean, they led me to Jack's king-sized bed and settled me under the covers, nestled between them. I must have drifted off and I came to sometime later to the feel of my pussy being licked.

They were both awake and had taken it upon themselves to wake me up nice and slow. Jack's lips were on my breasts, his fingers gave one nipple a little pinch as he sucked the other into his mouth and tugged. They must have heard my sharp inhale because I heard Sam's low laugh from between my parted thighs where his tongue teased the folds of my pussy, so lightly it could only be described as torture.

He flicked out his tongue to lick my clit. "You want more of that?"

I answered with a moan and Jack responded by sucking harder on my nipple. Sam waited until I was begging before he gave me what I really wanted. Sliding up, he pushed his cock into my throbbing pussy, filling me up like he knew I needed. His strokes were devastatingly slow and shallow, and I whimpered for more, faster.

"You want me to make you come, doll?"

Yes! God, yes. I needed it.

"You want Jack to help?"

I nodded my head, or at least I tried to but ended up thrashing it back and forth as I grabbed Sam's ass, urging him to give me more.

"Easy, doll. We'll give you what you need. Tonight."

"Every night," Jack added, cupping my breast. "You're ours, sweetness."

And oh, did they take care of me. Over and over and over again. Later, we fell asleep like that, with me nestled in the middle.

Exactly where I belonged.

WANT MORE?

———

Read an excerpt from Claim Me Hard, book 2 in the Bridgewater County Series!

———

CLAIM ME HARD - EXCERPT

$\mathcal{H}$ANNAH

Their hands were on me. Yes, *their*. Two sets of large, rugged palms skidded over my bare skin, awakening every nerve ending in their paths. I could feel them, one on each side of me. I was sandwiched between two hard, well-muscled bodies, their erect cocks pressing against my hips. They wanted me, that was obvious.

But two men? I was a doctor. My social life consisted of an hour-long dinner break at midnight between trauma cases. The only variation in my wardrobe was whether I would wear green or blue scrubs with my white doctor's coat. My makeup had expired in the second year of med school and my hair hadn't been in anything but a ponytail to keep it out of my face for just as long.

I couldn't lure one man in my bed, let alone two. Well, I'd lured one asshole, but it had never been like this. Never been hot and needy, frantic and...naughty. One found the back of my knee, pulled me wide. The other matched actions so I was on my back, my legs spread. With their hands holding me open, I was at their mercy, available for whatever they wanted to do. And that included a finger very gently circling the top of my clit.

"You're soaking wet through your panties," the voice said, dark and rough. He seemed very pleased that I was aroused for him. I *was* wet; I could feel the silk cling to my folds. Rough stubble abraded my neck as I was kissed. Angling my head, I offered him better access.

I felt a tug at my hip, then heard the rip of my dainty underwear. That was my only feminine concession. Fancy undies. That pair was now trashed, just a wisp of discarded fabric, but I didn't care. A guy just ripped my panties off. I was *not* going to complain.

"Ever had two men before?" The words were whispered in my ear. It was the second man, his voice rougher, if that were possible. Goosebumps rose on my flesh at the sound.

I shook my head, bumped his forehead.

"You're going to love it."

A hand brushed over my bare nipple and I gasped. My body was so responsive, the tip hardening immediately. I arched my back, eager for more. That light caress was not enough.

Yes, I was going to love it.

A finger circled my entrance, round and round, but not slipping inside.

"Please," I begged. I knew what I wanted and it was them, it was everything they would give me.

"Patience. Good girls get just what they deserve," the voice said as his finger slipped inside.

"Yes!"

All at once, I was chilled, the gentle and ardent hands were gone. I no longer felt them surrounding me. I was alone. It was dark and instead of feeling desired, I felt dirty. Scared. Exposed.

"Bad girls get just what they deserve."

That voice.

Oh god. I knew that voice.

It hadn't been the voices of the other men. No, it was Brad.

He was mad. Irate. I cringed, curling up into a ball to protect myself.

I smelled the familiar, cloying cologne. "You're mine. You'll never get away from me."

I sat bolt upright in bed, gasped as I struggled against the sheets tangled about my legs, trying to get away.

A dream.

God, it was all a dream.

No hot men. No Brad.

I was in my new apartment over the diner. Alone. Free from Brad, but hardly free.

I was covered in sweat, my t-shirt damp, my breath coming in harsh gasps. My skin quickly chilled, my nipples hardening. My pussy ached, remembering the way I'd been touched in the dream. My hand slid down beneath the covers, beneath my panties. I was wet and needy from the dream. I wanted those fingers getting me off, even with the crazy idea of it being a threesome. Insane. Unreal. But it had been nothing but a dream. A hot, sweaty dream, but Brad ruined it. Not just in my sleep, but in my waking hours, too.

He ruined everything.

I might have fled LA and his cruel fists, but the voice in my dream had been too true.

I would never get away from him.

Read Claim Me Hard now!

GET A FREE BOOK!

JOIN MY MAILING LIST TO BE THE FIRST TO KNOW OF NEW RELEASES, FREE BOOKS, SPECIAL PRICES AND OTHER AUTHOR GIVEAWAYS.

http://freeromanceread.com

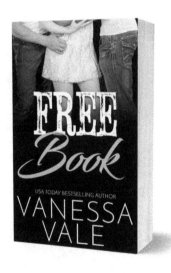

ABOUT THE AUTHOR

Vanessa Vale is the *USA Today* Bestselling author of over 50 books, sexy romance novels, including her popular Bridgewater historical romance series and hot contemporary romances featuring unapologetic bad boys who don't just fall in love, they fall hard. When she's not writing, Vanessa savors the insanity of raising two boys, she's figuring out how many meals she can make with a pressure cooker. While she's not as skilled at social media as her kids, she loves to interact with readers.

www.vanessavaleauthor.com

ALSO BY VANESSA VALE

Grade-A Beefcakes

Sir Loin Of Beef

T-Bone

Tri-Tip

Porterhouse

Skirt Steak

Small Town Romance

Montana Fire

Montana Ice

Montana Heat

Montana Wild

Montana Mine

Steele Ranch

Spurred

Wrangled

Tangled

Hitched

Lassoed

Bridgewater County Series

Ride Me Dirty

Claim Me Hard

Take Me Fast

Hold Me Close